About the Author

Bastian Gregory was born in 1997 and spent a happy childhood in Singapore, Hong Kong and Denmark. He went on to study creative writing in the UK. He was a wild and free thinker, a kind, gentle son and brother and a good friend to many. Bastian had Aspergers Syndrome and suffered from depression. He left us just after his twenty-third birthday to be, in his own words, reincarnated 'as a cosmic tree with solar winds and alien doves rushing through my branches'. He leaves behind this book and a collection of poems.

Aboard the Time Line

Bastian Gregory

Aboard the Time Line

Nightingale Books

VANGUARD PAPERBACK

© Copyright 2021
Bastian Gregory

A CIP catalogue record for this title is
available from the British Library.

ISBN 978-1-80016-001-9

Vanguard Press is an imprint of
Pegasus Elliot MacKenzie Publishers Ltd.
www.pegasuspublishers.com

First Published in 2021

Vanguard Press
Sheraton House Castle Park
Cambridge England

Printed & Bound in Great Britain

Dedication

To Bastian Gregory in loving memory from Mor, Dad, May & Luke. An amazing and talented free spirit.

Acknowledgements

Thanks to my sister May for the illustrations; thanks to my parents and Jacqui & Andy Parsons for helping bring this book to a wider audience.

Chapter 1
An Especially Dull Maths Class

Tick Tock
Tick Tock
Tickety Tock
Tick Tock

For a just a moment, Pete thought the clock had gone tickety tock rather than tick tock. Alas no, it had just gone tick tock again. His imagination was playing tricks on him. Twenty long minutes were left until the end of his maths lesson, but he was already going mad with boredom. The clock making odd sounds was not even the worst of it. He felt a distant awareness that what was being said was probably important somehow, but the teacher's words had blended with the background noise of the room. There was a boy behind him clicking his pen incessantly and another group gossiping at the back who had mastered the art of whispering and messing around with a subtlety that went unnoticed by  the teacher but not the other students. Pete stared at the people around him, wondering if perhaps striking up a conversation would make the time pass quicker, but he had not mastered that art. Whenever he stepped out of line in class, it seemed it got noticed, maybe he just hadn't quite figured the right volume to whisper yet, or the speed to look down at his task, just as the teacher's gaze lifted from their scribbled examples. No, he would just have to sit there and eye the clock menacingly, making sure it wouldn't play any more tricks on his senses. Another twenty or thirty "Tick Tocks" went by. Pete started to feel his eyes getting heavier and heavier.

With a start, he awoke and immediately groaned, as he realised not even a minute had gone by. Then, he noticed something strange was afoot. For a start, no one noticed his unintentionally loud groan. The clock wasn't even tick-tocking any more, it was as if time stood still. Hang on, the teacher wasn't talking any more, in fact, neither was the group at the back, and the pen wasn't clicking. He looked behind him, and the boy's pen and hand had frozen mid-click. Now he was really worried that he might actually be going mad. It seemed everything around him stood completely still. Then came an unexpected knocking on the door, neither loud nor quiet and rather slow. Looking around to find everything still frozen, Pete supposed he should answer the door. He stood up and took a moment to bask in the ability to wander around in class, without attracting the teacher's glare. As an experiment, he let himself think out loud.

"If I am going mad, I might as well enjoy it."

Sure enough, there was no answer or even movement from anyone else in the class. There was a knocking on the door again as Pete approached. From the other side, a muffled ancient-sounding voice politely inquired, "Excuse me, there would not happen to be anyone within, would there?"

Pete opened the door and his muddled head, already struggling to come to grips with the frozen classroom behind him, was suddenly bombarded with a lot more to take in. His school corridor had been replaced with a wild jungle, there were huge ferns everywhere and the loud hum of a million different noises combined. What's more, in front of him was hunched an actual, living dinosaur! The creature was about Pete's height, with a pair of glasses balanced precariously on his long raptor snout. He was sat up on his hind legs, knocking, revealing quite a large pot-belly. The door opening seemed to give him a fright, as he jumped with an expression of extreme surprise, almost losing the tall black hat he wore.

"Why goodness gracious, hello," said the dinosaur in a blustering voice that reminded Pete of his granddad. "My name is Reginald, Reginald Raptor. Pleased to make your acquaintance, young one. Now would you explain what you and your large box are doing here? I must say, it was a terrible shock, more consideration should be taken when you decide to appear in places."

"Um…" Pete didn't know where to start. The confusion left him speaking almost automatically, the manners he had been taught took over his tongue, despite all the strangeness.

"My name is Pete, pleased to meet you. I'm sorry if I bothered you, but I'm really not sure what is happening right now. I was just sitting in a very dull maths class dozing a bit and then you appeared?" Reginald cocked his head sideways in an inquisitive glance.

"Well, my boy, I do believe I know what has happened, you must be from the real world. Come to visit, have you? We do get so few from there."

"No really, I was just in class, bored out of my mind when…"

"AHA! That's it then, what a terrible state, terrible, terrible."

Pete was baffled by this interruption. "What?"

Reginald continued: "You said it, my boy, you've clearly been bored out of your mind."

He turned and cast his short claw across the jungle behind him. Proudly proclaiming, "Welcome to Outermind."

Chapter 2
Outermind

Pete was very confused about what exactly was going on. First, everything had frozen, now in front of him stood a very odd jovial raptor, who was heartily welcoming him to a place he was sure didn't exist. Who had ever heard of a place called Outermind? This must just be a figment of his imagination. Surely? And how was he supposed to get back? Was there a way out of this strange dream that certainly did not feel like any of the dreams he had before?

"Umm, Reginald?"

"Call me Reggie, my boy."

"Okay, Reggie, do you know how I can find my way back? To my world, or time or wherever I was before everything froze?"

"Hmm, no not a clue. But..." Reggie went on to boisterously explain that he understood not much more than Pete did about what had happened but that he knew someone who might.

"My friend Philosophocles talked a bunch about being bored out of one's mind, but he does a lot of talking about a lot of things and I don't always do as much listening you see... Would be good for us to catch up anyway. Come along then, I'll take you to him. If you're new here, you'll need a guide."

Very puzzled, thoughts still awash with questions of whether or not he was dreaming, Pete hesitantly thanked the old dinosaur for his cheerful offer. With that, he left the frozen classroom behind and followed Reggie into the primeval jungle that grew thicker and wilder than any forest Pete had seen.

Along the way, Reggie regaled Pete with tales from his home-time in Outermind. It seemed he knew every tree and root and neighbour, constantly pausing his stories to tell Pete that this area was where the such-and suches lived and what they had been up to. As he digressed, Reggie would often forget his old story completely, starting a new one involving those he mentioned. He lamented the days when he was young and could have offered Pete a ride on his back and run as fast as anything.

"You don't seem all that old," Pete said, partly out of politeness and a little bit of excitement at the opportunity to ride on a real live dinosaur.

"But of course I am, silly, I am a dinosaur after all, we are very old, Peter, my boy. Even the youngest of us are at least sixty-five million years you know, oh how my bones creak, why I am almost a fossil."

Reggie looked off into the distance sullenly, Pete took a moment to remember how many zeroes were in a million and while trying to comprehend such a large number, Reggie turned back to his stories, his loud, joyful, self had returned. "Ah well, not much to be done about this now. Everything and everyone has its time, you know. Now where was I, ah yes; well some pterodactyls had offered to take me flying…"

They continued their walk, Reggie continuing the story of his first flight, involving the surprise appearance of a strange vehicle (which Philosophocles, had later told him was a helicopter) that had created some turbulent gusts in the wind around it, and how he had never liked heights since. Along the way, Pete saw all sorts of creatures, some that he recognised from drawings; like the brontosaurus and triceratops, and many more that he did not. He was looking with his own eyes at the sorts of strange and wonderful beasts that he had read about and seen in books, but never in his wildest imagination thought he would see alive, seemingly going about their normal daily business.

"Where does this Fisocles live?"

"Phil-o-soph-o-cles, Peter, and he lives in Ancient Greece, of course! Now, that is quite a long way from here in the Cretaceous period, we certainly won't be walking all the way. We will have to take the train to get to him."

Pete was more confused than ever, searching his head, trying to make sense of it all. Surely they didn't have trains in Ancient Greece, let alone way back when dinosaurs existed, long before humans came along?

"But how will a train take us through time?"

"Ah, so you do know it, my boy! Yes, it should just be a few short stops on the Time Line."

"The timeline? But isn't that just a thing we use to make it easier to understand what happened when and sort out all the different dates in textbooks?"

"No, no that's a timeline, this is The Time Line. It's our longest and oldest train system and it's the best way to get around in Outermind... well, I say around. It's been undergoing maintenance for a while, so for now it only goes one way. It makes getting back to where you came from a bit of an inconvenient hassle, partly why I haven't been to Ancient Greece in some time... Very odd, actually, when you wonder where all the carriages end up going after you get off... and the "maintenance", well, it feels like it has been going on forever, but I have never seen any workers... Never mind, my thoughts and memories feel fuzzy and strange whenever I think about that. Let's keep walking, it's not far now."

With a few reinvigorated hops, Reggie bounded off towards a strangely ordinary-looking train station, given its location in a place of such wonder. The odd familiarity of a modern structure, amongst the unfamiliarity of primordial earth, left Pete wondering about the logistics of dinosaurs on trains and where exactly the Cretaceous period fitted into all this. He was sure he remembered it being a time and not a place, although he supposed all times had places within them... or did all places have times within them?

Walking up the grey concrete stairs that sprouted out of the jungle like another odd, long-extinct plant, they got onto the platform that would take them onwards to Ancient Greece. Just as Reggie said, all the trains only seemed to go one way, so finding the right platform was not hard, although they make sure to take the fast line on Reggie's recommendation.

On the platform, there was a whole host of strange and wonderful passengers.

Pete stuck close to Reggie as he meandered effortlessly through the crowd of all shapes and sizes. He almost bumped into a tall stack of tiny hats that reached up to Pete's nose before he heard "Watch it" being squeaked at him from a very small person down by his shoes who was wearing the excessive amount of hats. "Sorry," he quickly muttered and promptly bumped into the back of a woolly mammoth, the  gargantuan, tusked creature turned around and rolled its eyes as Pete scurried back to Reggie. He had also had a small collision and was humbly apologising to a couple of purple badgers, whose bags he had knocked over with his unwieldy tail.

"Stick close, Peter, we would not want to get separated from each other here, it seems the next train shall be along in a couple of minutes." A bird flying by stopped to greet Reggie while they waited.

"Who was that?"

"My cousin, Robin."

"Cousin?"

"Birds and dinosaurs, my boy, same sort of face, can't you tell? We are related, didn't you know? You might even some know lizards, snakes and other reptiles in my distant family!"

Before Pete could answer, the train stopped at the station with a massive screech. Strange, as Pete hadn't noticed it approach. The driver leaned out the window and yelled:

"All aboard the Time Line! This is the fast line, so we will have a bit of a jump to our next stop in Sumeria. Please ensure all baggage and small children are properly secured."

Chapter 3
The Time Line

Stepping onto the train was no less of an assault on the senses than being on the platform had been. In fact, the enclosed space was full to the brim with so many odd passengers, it made Pete realise how much he stood out. There was a rhinoceros standing on its hind legs speaking to a small waddle of penguins, each wearing two monocles, not just one; surely spectacles would be simpler? There was what looked to be a marching band, dressed all in matching tartan taking up three rows; however, their instruments seemed to take the place of their ears, sprouting out of their heads. Amongst all the madness, Pete discovered there was not a single ordinary-looking person, creature, or thing on this train matching his memory of the normal world. Even the handholds were pink and green, striped and fluffy. The confusion was exciting, although a bit of fright also arose that quickly reminded him how glad he was for Reggie's assistance.

No sooner did the doors close, and Pete and Reggie squeeze into some almost non-existent space than the entire train was rocked by an enormous yank. Pete struggled to hold himself upright, then started feeling a sinking sensation that was making him very queasy. He thought he should try to settle his stomach by looking out the window, as that is what he normally did if he felt unwell.

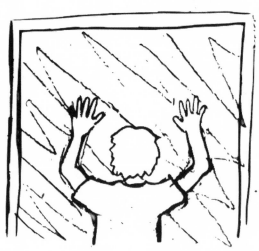

But this in itself was difficult, as he could only glimpse it through a needle-thin gap in between body parts and suitcases that blocked him from the window. Big mistake! Nothing was as expected! He noticed the train was in fact not going along any tracks, as it had initially appeared at the station, but falling rapidly through the air. He tugged on Reggie's shoulder in utter panic, exclaiming that they were falling, and shouldn't they try and do something?

Reggie simply laughed and said, "Well, of course we are falling, did you not hear the conductor saying there would be a bit of jump? There are about 65 million years between the Cretaceous period and where we're going. You did not think we would go all that way along tracks, did you? That would take way to long! Relax, Peter, things start happening closer together once recorded history starts and the ol' Time Line isn't so reliant on palaeontology to figure out where we are."

"But... but... trains can't fly."

"You really will have to stop saying but. Ask why instead. There's a far better chance you will get a good answer that way, and you are less likely to be so confused, my boy. Of course, trains can't fly, it's the fast line, there is a lot between us and Ancient Greece, so it jumped," said Reggie as if that made perfect sense out of all the confusion in Pete's mind.

A fellow passenger took an interest in Pete's curiosity, taking the time to explain how this specific train in the Time Line was saving on heating expenses by jumping over the Ice Age, and explaining that this was also why there were so many wearing many coats, as they would have to walk back to the Ice Age to visit some family. The friendly small talk with the something under the pile of coats distracted Pete from their perpetual descent. That is, until a massive clang and grumble of "oofs," "pardons," and "watch its" denoted the train landing back on its rails and the carriages subsequently shaking.

"Well, that went better than expected," said Pete, just managing to remain standing, supported by Reggie's tail.

"That's the spirit, Peter, not long now," Reggie said boisterously, his support echoed by a muffled whoop from within the coats.

"Well, a flying train certainly beats maths class! I'd forgotten that's where I'm meant to be," said Pete.

"Not flying, Peter, my boy, jumping. Now that would be ridiculous. I really will have seen everything when trains start flying." Reggie's odd logic somehow comforted Pete, who thought he had heard of trains flying along magnetic rails.

But before he could mention that to Reggie, the voice of the conductor rang out to tell the passengers that they would be stopping in Sumeria shortly and that taking any souvenirs was highly discouraged, as they had met many people calling themselves "archaeologists" who had been digging around, looking for these so-called souvenirs, far in the future. As they pulled up at the station, their many-coated acquaintance thanked them for the conversation and began the trek back towards where they came. "What is your name, good passenger?" called Reggie after them. "Wallace," came the muffled return from the coats.

"Reginald Raptor, pleased to have met you," he replied, tipping his hat out of the train in a farewell salute. Meanwhile, Pete wondered how absolutely sweltering it must be under all those coats, in the desert surroundings of the Sumerian station, and how it would be a long trek back to the Ice Age, only now considering that it wasn't his nerves but a sudden cold which had caused his goosebumps near the end of the terrifying jump.

Well, perhaps a combination of those two, he admitted to himself.

Before he could consider these thoughts any further, the conductor recited: "All aboard the Time Line! Please ensure… etc.," once more, and that their next stop was to be Ancient Greece.

Chapter 4
Not so Ancient Greece

Luckily, after the last stop, the train carriage was less full, and Pete could finally get a good look outside the window. As opposed to the open sky he glimpsed earlier, this time the view was marvellous. Pete started regretting how quickly it all passed by, feeling an urge to explore this wild world he had found himself in. As they approached Ancient Greece, Pete's face was glued to the landscape whizzing past outside. It reminded him of time-lapse footage of growing plants that he remembered seeing in science class. As the train sped along, foundations and villages became buildings and cities, going from wood to stone to marble. Elaborate creations of architecture began to spring up, the Great Pyramids of Giza began emerging up on the horizon and grew and grew, until they passed them, and they disappeared back over the opposite horizon.

Pete tried to do a quick estimate of just how fast the train must have been speeding along for such huge structures to zip past so quickly. It was impossible. He was quickly driven to give up as beautiful white marble structures with grand pillars came into sight. These, and the olive trees that were haphazardly arranged in small orchards around the towns they passed, reminded Pete of their intended destination. Excited that he recognised it, he pulled on Reggie's scaled arm exclaiming, "We're here soon, this is Ancient Greece, I recognise it!"

"Oh, have you been before?"

"No of course not! Just from my history lessons and books and… never mind."

Pete trailed off, he felt there was no point, there was a lot he had to adjust to in this strange place, and he might as well focus on listening and experiencing rather than trying to explain what life was like back in his normal world.

The now-familiar voice of the conductor announced

their stop, and Pete and Reggie clambered their way over the snoring back of a large bear who had decided to take a brief hibernation right in the way of the door.

They managed to get off just in time, and Pete looked back over the tracks from the way they came. They were near the top of a large round hill that the city had been built on. The vantage of being on top of the hill did not help, however, the tracks went on and on in both directions, giving up no secrets as to where they would lead. Reggie took a long, deep breath of air and said, "There is no place like the Acropolis. Sweet sun, olives, art and drama, the weather, architecture, oh the lovely people and the knowledge, aaah, the knowledge."

Reggie's entire body seemed to melt into the floor with joy. He clearly liked this place very much. He strolled forward purposefully as if wanting to take in every little detail.

Momentarily forgotten, Pete struggled to rush after him as they ascended the shallow incline leading up to the largest and most grand amongst all the buildings that stood atop the hill, overlooking the city. The hustle and bustle of early civilisation were all around. They passed a fantastic market where open stalls were propped up around each other, vendors crying out to be heard amidst it all, plenty of people preoccupied with the buying and selling of wares used in the lives of ancient times.

"Olives, olives, finer olives would not be found in Olympus!"

"Sweet Dionysus wine, made only from local grapes!"

These were just some of the cries one could hear coming from the marketplace.

The crowd finally slowed Reggie down enough that Pete could catch up. They now made their way together through the bulging bustle of commerce, cautious not to bump into anything that could set off a chain reaction of toppling. Relieved, they finally made it through only to come upon more stairs. Pete groaned as he had already felt his legs getting tired. Noticing this, Reggie consoled him.

"Why the House of Learning is just up here, my boy, not long to go now. Philosophocles is likely holding a lecture within."

He then gave him a jolly pat on the back, or at least he tried, having arms as short as he did, meant that he couldn't reach very far. Pete was worried upon hearing House of Learning, it reminded him of school and did not sound promising. But he had already experienced so much that he didn't understand and so many strange and wonderful things, that perhaps doing a little bit of learning in Ancient Greece might not be so bad after all. After all, the things that he did with Reggie seemed to be a lot more fun than they had at school and he had certainly learned a lot. They commenced climbing the steps up to the top of the Acropolis.

Chapter 5
Philosophocles

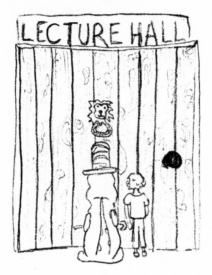

Walking between some marvellous pillars that were easily six or seven-times Pete's height, they came to a large wooden door that said Lecture Hall on it. They opened it up, it was not at all what Pete was expecting. If this was supposed to be some sort of school, well, there was a lot more chaos than Pete was used to in his school. No structure, no timetables. Everywhere you could see, there were people loudly reading off scripts they held in front of them, with wild gestures garnering applause from their peers. Others were eccentrically and passionately displaying and describing their artwork of any form to anyone who would listen. There were inventors holding aloft their contraptions of greatly varying viability and usefulness. Doctors pointing sticks to charts depicting various bits of the body and how to "cure" them. Some of these cures looked very suspicious indeed. Geniuses mingled with the insane and everyone in between, such that it became very hard to tell the difference. It was an extraordinary scene to behold, and one that totally overwhelmed the senses.

Amongst all this commotion a figure in a robe, haphazardly chequered with patches of many different colours, and a long white beard combed into two wispy forks and huge eyebrows that almost matched, extending significantly over the sides of his face, stumbled into the room. He was barely managing to carry a very tall, and what looked very heavy, podium. He then clumsily placed the podium at the back of the hall and proceeded to clamber up onto it. Thereupon he perched, looking regal and ridiculous all at once. Slowly the demonstrations and performances around him ceased what they were doing, as people began to turn towards him. Their example swept through the room, until even the people by the entrance

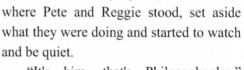 where Pete and Reggie stood, set aside what they were doing and started to watch and be quiet.

"It's him, that's Philosophocles," Reggie whispered to Pete.

Philosophocles gazed out into the room, saying nothing and just observing as the last of the loud marvellous swell of ideas came to an awed silence. There was an awkwardly long time after the noise was gone where he and the room all sat in expectant stillness. There was a cough from the crowd splitting the quiet. Then another. Another minute went by where there was no sound, just silence. Someone near the front broke the stillness with a stifled giggle. Suddenly, the strange little bearded man exploded into action with a very forceful and sudden.

"HELLO!"

He then gave the crowd a casual wave, as if he had just greeted someone across the street.

Then began his speech. It was very odd and long and confusing. It seemed obvious that none of the audience really understood more than a small fraction of what he had to say. Despite this, they were enthralled and totally enraptured by the words. Philosophocles's wild gestures and movements around his tall narrow podium mimicked performers or street artists that Pete occasionally saw gathered around supermarkets on busy days. This kept Pete's attention, much more so than any of his teachers back in his normal school were able to. So, despite not understanding much, he made out parts of the rant. It consisted mostly of a lot of unanswerable questions:

"What are we?"

"What aren't we?"

"What were we?"

"What will we?"

"What won't we?"

Things carried on in this fashion for some time, Philosophocles asked himself a question, then answered himself with another, and then another, until he, Pete, Reggie and the entire audience became thoroughly confused but completely captured by this one-man argument of inquiries.

Some time into the speaking, Reggie began to nod off to sleep. Pete looked over at him. The sight of an ageing fat dinosaur falling asleep was both adorable and quite funny. He balanced between his tail and belly and seemed to be quite trained in sleeping without others noticing. That is until his loud snoring began with a growl that made Pete's hair stand on end. With all the prehistoric power in the aged raptor's body, a great rumbling snore went through the crowd. Even Philosophocles, who had spoken tirelessly for some time now, stopped as the vibrations coming from this terrible roar across the hall shook his podium, forcing him to cling to it to avoid falling.

"That can only mean one thing," Philosophocles said, as soon as he regained his balance.

"REGINALD!" he called out in a sharp, loud bark. He then began clambering down the podium and moving through the crowd towards the epicentre of the great noise.

Next to Pete, Reggie stirred awake, confusedly looking around as all eyes were on him, aghast at the noise he had unwittingly produced.

"Oh dear, Peter, I do seem to have nodded off and caused quite a fuss," he said.

He sheepishly muttered pardons and apologies to the onlookers, just in time to be tackled into a hug by a very excited Philosophocles.

"REGGIE! It has been far too long," he shouted again

while clinging onto the befuddled raptor.

"PHIL! Good to see you, old man," the dinosaur replied.

More cheerful greetings were exchanged, and Reggie introduced Pete to Philosophocles.

Once Philosophocles was informed that there was an interesting conundrum that Pete needed help to solve, he lost interest in his lecture and the crowd; immediately intrigued by this new problem, he invited them to join him in his office. Almost as an afterthought while they were leaving the room, he turned back to the crowd, still waiting expectantly, as if this had all been part of some plan to make a point and yelled, "OKAY I'M DONE, THANK YOU!"

With that announcement, they walked off into a corridor; behind them, they heard a moment's pause and then a rustle as if the whole hall exhaled at once and people began returning to their business. The entire audience felt a lot more confused now than when they had entered the hall, but that was partially the point and they were used to this, so no one really minded. Except perhaps the man who questioned the existence of one of the exit doors and bumped his head walking straight into it. He concluded; yes, for at least that moment his head came into contact, the door did very much exist.

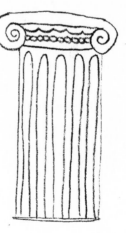

Chapter 6
Answers?

Phil led them into his "office" if it could be called that. A kaleidoscope of colours and shapes was perhaps more accurate. Nothing in there seemed to make much sense or have any discernible logic as to why it was there. There was, amongst other weird things, a desk for example, but it was bright orange and glued to the ceiling.

"Sit, sit, make yourselves comfortable, please."

Pete looked around for anything that could reasonably be called a chair with no success. Failing that, he found a patch of floor that didn't look too strange or bumpy and sat cross-legged. Meanwhile, Reggie leaned back on his tail and Phil perched himself on a small bar hanging in the centre of the room like a tiny trapeze.

"Well, well, will? Well? Won't? So, I hear there is a mystery afoot? An unsolved appearance?"

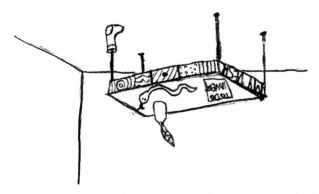

"Yes, erm I was just sitting in class when suddenly everything just stopped, and there was a knocking at the door. I opened the door to see Reggie and a jungle instead of my normal school corridor," explained Pete.

At this moment, Reggie perked up and described the curious circumstances that had led them here. "So, Peter said to me that he had been bored out of his mind, which was obviously how he came to be with us, but now he is looking for a way to get back again, and that's when I thought you might help."

At this, Phil gasped.

"Bored out of your mind? Oh, how terribly awful and awfully terrible."

"Oh, well I suppose it isn't great. It happens often enough though. I'm used to it," responded Pete, with a confused smile at Phil's outpouring of sympathy.

At the mention of being used to boredom, Phil looked as if he was being brought to tears. Before Pete could even ask Philosophocles if he could help or if he knew what had happened, he leapt off his bar and punched the air decisively while saluting with his other hand.

"Your cause is worthy, Sir Peter-of-not-this-mind, I pledge to you I will help you fight your boredom!"

Pete was a bit startled at this sudden and emotional display from Philosophocles.

"No, that's not the problem. I am used to that. I just want to know how to get back home."

In another sudden transformation, Phil went from being triumphant and ceremonial back to excitable and erratic, speaking very quickly about things Pete couldn't even try to understand, barely picking out words like "possibility spheres" and "quantum something-or-another". Then he clapped his hands together and beamed a massive smile at Pete.

"So?" said Pete expectantly.

"I have no idea," Phil replied, still smiling a broad cheerful grin.

Understandably, this upset Pete quite a bit as his hopes for returning home seemed dashed. He started thinking of all the things he would never see again and wished he had paid more attention to his world and what he was being taught and not seen it all in such a dull way. Filled with regret and not a little amount of fear and uncertainty, he felt a tear reaching his eye.

Reggie wrapped his tail around him, noticing his change in mood significantly before Phil, who was still beaming at the idea of something he didn't have the answer to. Finally realising the impact his answer had, Philosophocles quickly consoled Pete.

"Don't worry, don't worry, worry not, Peter. For while I don't know how to get you back, I do know you will get back. That's how Outermind works. Also, I already have a cunning hypothesis. Don't lose hope. I will help you, and I'm sure Reggie would be more than happy to come with us."

Pete looked up at him and recovered a little bit. Having something to focus on besides the possibility of getting stuck in Outermind, combined with Reggie's comforting tail, calmed him.

Phil continued, "Well, seeing as you have been bored out of your mind, what I think is that we have to 'unbore' you back into your mind, perhaps? Which is why I will take you on an adventure through Outermind. And once we see all there is to be seen and all there isn't to be not seen, I think the answer might reveal itself. And the main point is that you will be learning and experiencing things that cannot possibly be boring, a proper adventure is what you need! Besides, seems like good fun. Are you with me?"

Pete agreed as it seemed his only option, although admittedly he was also curious as to what more this strange world had in store for him. He supposed he didn't want to go back to maths class right away regardless. Reggie stated that he would stick by him until he found a way back. At this display of kindness, the tear that he had almost shed earlier came tumbling out, and he quickly turned his head to wipe it away and shield his overwhelmedness.

He sniffled, "Thank you, both of you are very kind."

"Well then, what are we waiting for? Time is ticking, or is it tocking?" Phil said, oblivious to Pete's little display of emotion.

"Back to the Time Line then. Oh, all the times and places we could go: Rome, the middle ages, feudal Japan. This is a tough choice, how are we going to organise ourselves and which might be the best places to visit?"

Chapter 7
An Adventure for Adventure's Sake

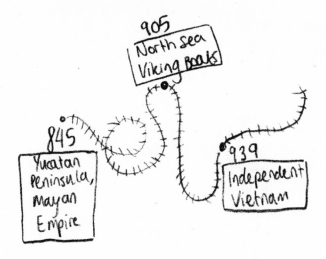

Phil continued to mutter suggestions to himself all the way back through the Acropolis. He was hopping ahead unsteadily, as he seemed to change his motions every five steps or so, from jogs to bounds, to swaggers, he led the odd trio with wild exuberance. This left Pete and Reggie to discuss the viability of his plan.

"I don't mean to sound rude but are you certain he will be any help?" asked Pete.

"Well, with Phil around, the last thing I can be of anything, is certain," replied Reggie.

"But don't let his eccentricity deter you, he is quite possibly the cleverest person there ever was. He cannot resist a good problem, and you have given him quite a tricky one, which means he will put his mind to it until it is solved. I'm sure you will be home in no time."

"I guess so. Thanks again, Reggie. I would be very lost if it weren't for your help."

"Think nothing of it, Peter. I'm always happy to help someone who needs it. Besides, you aren't the only one for whom boredom strikes. Not much for an old fossil like me to do these days, I sometimes feel increasingly unsure of what I am and if I really belong anywhere any more. But now we're having an adventure and my mind is too busy racing with possibilities to worry about all that, so I should also thank you for your sudden appearance."

As they spoke, they approached the station just as a train was arriving. Phil leapt forth onto the platform, very suddenly and extravagantly welcoming all the visitors from the train arrival to Ancient Greece, to a mixture of surprise and awkward laughter at the friendly crazy man, who most of the passengers did not yet recognise. Little did they realise that, for many of them, his speeches were the reason they had come to Ancient Greece, and apart from this greeting, they would have missed the chance to see and hear him and his grand postulations. One woman, dressed in World War Two army fatigues recognised him, taking a quick picture with her massive black-and-white camera, turning heads as the crowd began to realise who had just passed them to step on the train.

"I guess we both have him to thank as well, he seems to have become quite the celebrity in these parts," Pete said to Reggie as they sheepishly followed behind the flamboyant, excited Phil.

"We will see, as long as he doesn't drive us mad first," Reggie replied, and they both laughed.

As they boarded the train, it seemed Phil had still not made up his mind on where the best time and place to have an adventure was. Finally, with the train starting and when they had found a comfortable seat amongst all the strange passengers, Pete summed up the courage to ask Phil:

"So... have you decided where we're getting off?"

"It's just so tough. There's something everywhere and nothing nowhere."

"Well, maybe just pick one randomly?"

"Brilliant, Peter, yes, absolutely brilliant."

"What no... I was just..." Pete let the sentence flow away.

With those words, he was suddenly lifted by Phil's arms holding him high above his head, with a strength that seemed far greater than his wiry frame allowed. Fortunately, the Time Line was built to contain passengers of all shapes and sizes, so there was no danger of him hitting the roof.

"Now, hold your hand up in the air and close your eyes."

By now, Pete was learning not to question anything he had been told in the time he had spent in Outermind, even more so when it was being said by Philosophocles. Additionally, the other passengers were staring at the odd display expectantly, so close his eyes and stick up his hand he did, feeling his fingers just touching the top of the carriage.

Below him, Pete felt Phil rapidly moving him back

and forth and spinning in circles. Just as Pete started to get dizzy and Phil's panting indicated he was actually tiring from lifting a person over his head, they stopped suddenly.

"Now whatever you do, don't move and slowly open your eyes."

Pete did so. Looking above him, he saw the list of stations the train would be stopping at, and a random squiggly path traced in the dust by his fingers.

"Now tell us where are you pointing? I can't see from down here."

Right where his finger was, in between 845 ~ Yucatan Peninsula, Mayan Empire and 939 ~ Independent Vietnam, was 905 ~ The North Sea, Viking boats.

"It says 905, The North Sea? Surely, we can't just stop in the sea, right?" said Pete.

"Ah, good choice, good choice. I've always wondered what that meant. I'm excited! Who knows? Maybe we'll stop in the ocean, on the ocean, or above the ocean. As long as we aren't by the ocean, or that may as well be on the land then," said Phil. Once again, his words seemed very confusing. Philosophocles was once again not necessarily making much sense to all those around him, although he obviously thought he was making sense himself. He lowered Pete down, already continuing his flow of speech, about how grand it all was and how excited he was to meet the Vikings, and whether it would be summer or winter and if it was winter he might not have the right clothes, although they wouldn't sail in winter, or would they? Typically, he continued for some time answering his questions with more questions and so on and so forth. Pete sat down, eager to distance himself from the emphatic Phil and all the attention he unwittingly drew from strangers. He settled in for the journey, trying to make heads or tails of what Phil was actually talking about.

"Vikings and the sea, eh? Suppose it's as good a place to start as any. I've never seen the ocean before," said Reggie with a hint of nervousness.

"Never?"

"Well the earth looked very different back in my day, all the continents were joined up in one called Pangea, so there was a lot less seaside and it was very far away from my forest," said Reggie.

"Well, until very recently, I had never met a dinosaur, been to Ancient Greece or even really gone out on my own adventure. Now I am glad to say that I have and I am. Maybe you'll enjoy the novelty of seeing the sea," Pete said with sudden wisdom.

Reggie considered this and smiled a toothy grin back at him, then the two compatriots stared out the window in comfortable solace. Meanwhile, Phil continued to rant and rave, not noticing the growing audience in the rest of the carriage.

Therefore, Reggie and Pete were the first to notice when suddenly the train tracks turned steeply downwards and plunged them underwater. The land was replaced by sea so fast that there was no time for Pete to either

panic or think that this was any stranger than anything that had gone before. Instead, Pete instantly glued himself to the new sights now available from the train-turned-submersible. Watching colourful corals and sea life of all sorts speeding past the window. The Time Line began to slow down and ascend once again, as it approached their next station. Slow enough for Pete to see a strange creature staring at him inquisitively. It was blubbery like a walrus, but it had fins like a shark and an oddly human face with freckles and bright red hair that looked very polygonal and edged in comparison with its sleek aqua-dynamic body.

Pete realised he was staring at this oddity and became keenly aware it was staring back. Breaking the tension between them in the only non-verbal way he could, he waved out of the window. As soon as he had done so, the creature looked frightened as if he had caused a huge shock and sped off into the murky blue abyss, disappearing almost instantly. Just as Pete watched the last of the bubbles that were the only trace of the creature's presence, the train rose out of the water. They came to a station that appeared identical to both the one in the Cretaceous and the Acropolis. However, this time it was floating in the middle of an ocean on a large pontoon, which seemed unanchored and unattached to anything but the rails. There was no land in sight, making the solitary grey station building drifting on the tide seem even more out of place and odd than the last two stations they had been to. (If that was even possible?) To solidify the alien weirdness of the station, it was surrounded by lavish wooden longships docked all around the platform, decorated to the extreme with coloured shields and painted sails. As the trio stepped onto the platform, they saw more ships arriving as others left their moorings. All of the ships carried groups of very large people, messy and dishevelled, clad in dark clothes and wrapped in furs, looking very understated, in stark contrast with the elaborately ornate ships they sailed.

Phil took Pete and Reggie by the shoulders and dragged them towards a newly arrived ship.

"If one is to find adventure where we are going, it's always a good place to start by talking to a local, especially if you are in the middle of the ocean." He added that as an afterthought, seeming to notice it for the first time. Reggie had very clearly noticed this, going a shade of very pale green (greener than he already was) at the lack of solid land. He was definitely uncomfortable at the unsteady rocking of waves and perturbed by what he thought was a rather unnatural phenomenon.

Chapter 8
Big Brigid and the Wikings

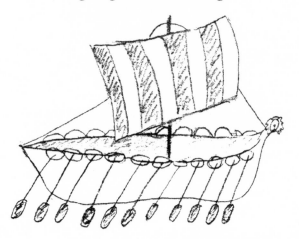

As they approached a newly arriving boat, they stopped dead in their tracks. When the boat neared the jetty, the largest person Pete had ever seen strode off the side of the boat, landing with a hefty thud in front of them. She towered above them, clad in wolfskin, with short yellow-blonde hair growing out from the top of a very harsh, tough-looking face. Pete was not exactly the tallest boy his age, and Reggie and Phil were both similar size to him. All three of them standing on each other's shoulders would not even have made it up to her head height.

Not to be dissuaded by this massive woman, after overcoming the momentary shock and awe, Phil introduced themselves to this giant.

"Hello, miss, my name is Philosophocles, and these are my compatriots Peter and Reginald. We are embarking on an adventure to cure this boy's boredom. Is there any chance you could perhaps recommend some tourist attractions in the near... vicinity?" He trailed off as if the notion that they were surrounded by water, and nothing but the water, had only then driven home. This was probably for the better, as the giant woman had only just noticed them, having to angle her face very far down to see them. Pete started feeling a little nervous as he noticed the ill-tempered look on her face and the threateningly sharp war axe she carried at her side. Then, with a booming voice she spoke with calm and rugged confidence, reserved only for the truly tough.

"Hello, little ones, I can see you aren't from here, you had best be on your way, the seas have not been safe around here recently. There are stories of cursed creatures under the waves."

"Cursed creatures?" Pete inquired, his curiosity overriding his sheepishness around this giant.

"Yes, stories of seal-like creatures with human faces, who sink ships and drown sailors. Certainly, no time for tourism."

Pete thought about the thing he had seen through the glass as they arrived. He thought it might be one of those creatures she was talking about, although it seemed more scared than threatening. Not at all like a creature that would sink ships and do evil things.

"I think I might have seen one on the way here, it didn't seem that bad though, I waved at it and it swam away looking scared," he said.

With that, the woman looked at him with interest, then she relaxed her posture, looking less confrontational and intimidating.

"If that is the case, then allow me to ask for your help. We have been trying to hunt these monsters for some time, and the only knowledge we have of them comes from the strange doctor we met, who warned us about them. If you would have the time to help, please come aboard and talk to him. We will make sure you share in the glory of our deeds."

The three of them looked nervously at each other, unsure of what to make of this rough group and whether a polite refusal was possible without upsetting them.

The woman must have noticed their trepidation because in that instant she laughed and introduced herself and her crew.

"Do not be scared, little travellers, we are warriors, that is true, but we only fight evil. I am Brigid "Big" Birgitteson, and these are my crew; the Wikings: Bort, Sven, Harald and Hilde and of course our mighty longship: The Whooping Wanderer. You are all three most welcome aboard."

At their introduction, the other massive people

onboard the ship whooped their own bellowing greetings, loudest of all was when their ship was named. The cheers for The Whooping Wanderer made the ship rumble and shake as if it were taking part in all the introductions.

After this raucous display, Pete agreed to come aboard and talk to this doctor. He became very aware of how small and soft his voice now felt, in comparison with the booming Wikings. Pete clambered up the wooden plank onto the ship, Phil close behind and Reggie on all fours clawing his way up, very cautious of falling into the water below, still looking as if he would be sick any moment. Once aboard, they immediately noticed the doctor. Reassuring at first was his height; he was as tall as they were, although he seemed comparatively small surrounded by the giants. Seeing that the doctor was barely taller than the bench he was working at made the trio feel slightly less out of place. He wore a lab coat that was far too large and as he turned around to face them, they were taken aback by his grimace, which seemed contorted into a constant expression of shock.

"Hello, I'm Pete. You wanted to talk to me?" he asked of the doctor, reaching out to shake his hand.

"All right, back off, back off. CAREFUL. Back off," came a sudden series of shouts from a man dressed in a modern dark-red suit and black tie, with dark black sunglasses just like Pete had seen people wearing at the beach on holiday. He stepped between the doctor and his outstretched hand. Despite being one of the few humans in Outermind that Pete had seen wearing modern clothing and looking somewhat "normal", the man had an oddly suspicious gaze, squinting his eyes at this new group, as if he was scanning for some kind of threat or concealed weaponry. Pete quickly felt deeply uncomfortable, revising his thought that there was anything ordinary about him.

"Calm down, uhm… Mr Lawyer. I have been assured of their intentions to share information with us. Keep an eye on them in case they attack though," came a shaky call from the doctor behind the glowering man. The doctor turned back to Pete, although never shook his outstretched hand, which he awkwardly lowered while the doctor spoke.

"My apologies, my lawyer here is most concerned for our continued wellbeing. He is a very worried man. I believe you had seen one of those awful monsters that these brave warriors are hunting?" said the doctor.

Pete looked nervously at the red-suited lawyer, who had stepped back but was still glaring daggers at him while he answered the doctor:

"Umm… yes, yes, I saw one on the way in. It didn't seem much like a monster, though, it looked scared and swam away really fast."

The lawyer shook his head and tutted:

"Oh, but they are the most dangerous beasts of all beneath the waves. I was just telling our brave cadre of monster slayers here. They have raided and terrorised the shores to the west and south for many years now. Please, if you could come with us and tell us the direction it swam in, you would be possibly saving many lives," said the doctor.

"They won't help, they don't care. You heard them earlier, they're just here for an adventure," said the lawyer with a sneer.

Before Pete could answer, Phil butted in with indignance, "Firstly, we shall absolutely help you, if that is what you desire. There is no need for such distrustful presumption of our ill will and apathy. And secondly, do not turn up your nose at the grand notion of adventure, one can have an adventure while helping others, you know. For an attorney in the employment of a doctor ostensibly trying to save lives, I find your attitude very lacking, good sir."

Phil was becoming increasingly forceful and looked like he would go on until Reggie gently calmed him down before he started ranting and raving.

Pete was very concerned about this pair on the ship. The lawyer was obviously very unfriendly, but the doctor had something off about him as well. He couldn't quite define what was bothering him about the pair of them, but something was not right.

Meanwhile, Brigid and the Wikings seemed to have grown tired of watching this conversation and were loudly arm-wrestling and shouting at the other end of the longship. They seemed a decent bunch, even if a bit rough and frightening at first. Besides, Phil had already all but made the decision for him, so he agreed to help. He pointed them off in the direction that he had seen the creature flee towards. Brigid and her crew wasted no time in casting off the ship, unfurling the sails and extending oars, with all the efficiency of born sailors who had many years of practice together. Instantly transforming themselves from a rowdy group of massive individuals to a machine-like group, as if they became part of the ship, all working together smoothly. The painted longship sped away from the Time Line station in the direction Pete had pointed. Their speed cutting white foam into the deep blue blanket of the sea stretched over the horizon.

Chapter 9
Feer and Diztruzt

It was not long before the floating platform faded out of sight. Brigid and her Wikings pulled massive oars through the water like it was air, their speed rivalling a motorboat. A storm was beginning to whip up around them. First came the drenching cold rain, a precursor to the mighty cracks of thunder which thumped against Pete's ears, finally followed by lightning which traced electrical cracks in the sky, shattering the thick grey clouds. The longship was being rocked around, and Pete and Phil were clinging onto things for dear life, while Reggie was being violently sick over the edge, occasionally stopping and turning to complain how he had left his cosy chair by the fire for this, and perhaps adventure wasn't all it was cracked up to be. The Wikings were totally unfazed, stoically rowing The Whooping Wanderer into the wind and the waves as if it were a dinghy on a still summer pond.

Despite the rain and spray, the doctor soon called out

to the others, saying he had sighted the monsters they were hunting. Sure enough, barely visible behind the blanket of weather were many more of the creatures Pete had seen earlier.

"They're preparing to attack!" shouted the strange doctor and his lawyer, cowering.

They didn't look like they were attacking, Pete thought, as everyone scrambled around him. Firstly, he didn't think that the creatures had noticed them yet through the storm, the motions they were making seemed more like gleeful wave-surfing than aggressive action. And secondly, they were not moving closer to them, but just focusing on their own playful movements in the water.

"Oh help! Get them! Get them! Throw the nets," squealed the doctor.

"Use the harpoons," seconded the lawyer.

Brigid stood majestically on the prow of the ship, braided blonde hair whipping in the wind, swirling a heavy net around her head. She looked like a statue of old medieval heroes and warriors Pete had seen in museums and old castles. But he had no time to admire this. The feeling that there was something wrong had followed him since boarding the ship, but now it manifested itself almost physically, as he felt driven to cry out.

"No! Wait!"

With two short swishes followed by a whooosh, the net was already away. Brigid's powerful arms casting accurately as it encircled the creatures with a splash. Pete's protests were stolen by the storm's wind, and he could only watch helplessly as these poor creatures writhed in the net, Brigid's hands rhythmically reeling them in. The Wikings stood ready beside her, each holding a wickedly barbed harpoon, poised to face whatever she brought in, their faces fearless and defiant. Next to Pete were the doctor and his lawyer, who moments ago were making a show of shivering with fear and panicking. Now whilst the Wikings were focused on their task, they let their masks down, and could not contain their glee and excitement at the prospect of capturing the creatures. The doctor was positively cackling with glee, his face a mask of lunacy and, despite the rain, the lawyer threw off his suit, spinning it around his head and as if himself catching an invisible foe in a paltry imitation of Brigid.

Pete turned to them and yelled, "What do you think you're doing? You know those aren't monsters!"

The doctor turned to him and smiled a mad grin. He then spoke slowly and solemnly.

"Of course they are, they are strange and scary. Besides this is my job and I enjoy it."

"I thought you were a doctor?" Pete replied.

The doctor continued solemnly, contrasting the barely concealed grins on both his and his lawyers face, "Of course, I am. Oh, we haven't been properly introduced, have we?"

The two then turned to each other and burst out in uncontrollable laughter, unable to hold it in any longer, the doctor's solemnity was apparently unbearably humorous.

Pete stared at them incredulously as they doubled over in front of him, slapping each other's legs and arms in laughter. He turned away, ignoring them and leapt up to stand next to Brigid, almost tumbling over the wet wooden railing into the rough black depths. In front of the boat, he noticed the struggling of the creatures getting weaker.

As they steadily got reeled in closer and closer, Pete saw the Wikings to either side of him raise their harpoons. There was not a lot of time to lose and he just had to stop this, he was as sure of this as he had ever been sure of anything in his life. He just knew that this was wrong!

He tugged and tugged as hard as possible at Brigid's arms, much to her annoyance, as she almost swatted him away.

"WHAT ARE YOU DOING?" she yelled at him, the wind doing nothing to dampen the volume of her shout or the terror that rose in Pete's chest. A second before it seemed Brigid would knock him back down onto the deck with a thump from her free hand, he gathered all the might in his body and forced it up through his throat in as mighty of a bellow as was possible:

"STOP! THEY AREN'T MONSTERS!"

For a moment, Brigid stopped tugging, giving the largest of the three creatures the chance to face its captors. Pete saw the look of recognition on the freckled face of a girl, from when they were underwater between windows on the Time Line. She looked up at him desperately and shouted at him for help, with a soft and blubbery voice.

"Please! I don't know what we've done. We are all just children, these are my little brothers. Help us!"

Brigid looked confused and turned to face the duplicitous doctor and lawyer. The two tricksters had moved to the back of the ship, putting as much distance as possible between themselves and the rest of the crew. Brigid seemed to have realised that something was wrong with the situation and in an unusually quiet and sad voice, Brigid spoke to the doctor and the lawyer.

"You used us... why?"

Clambering up some rigging to gain height, the doctor cast his gaze down upon them, now very menacing but with more than a hint of worry at the group of very angry faces staring. He pointed straight at Pete, quivering with what could have been terror or rage:

"YOU, you have stopped our tricks. How can a demon be expected to do his job with you meddling?"

"A demon?" Pete questioned, still confused at their motivations.

"I told you earlier, we have not been introduced properly. I am Dr Feer! And this is my good friend; the attorney of arrogance, the barrister of bafflement, counsellor of confusion; the detestable Diztruzt." He replied, reciting their names proudly as if he were a crier at a fairground.

The rain and lightning picked up as he spoke, and as he did, their faces twisted and deformed and formed again, into grim, very cruel and menacing masks.

Meanwhile, Brigid and her Wikings had gotten over the confusion at their betrayal and turned to face their true enemy, steadily closing the distance between them and the demons on the ship, scowling.

The two demons saw this and started squabbling amongst themselves. Feer was struggling to put Diztruzt between him and Brigid, pulling at his suit yelling, "We need to go, we need to go."

Diztruzt looked angrily back at "doctor" Feer and squinted his eyes at him in a quiet argument lost to the whining winds. Suddenly, just as the heavily armed Wikings were about to reach them, Diztruzt pulled off his suit jacket and flapped it in the wind. Suddenly he was away, being blown upwards by the storm, using his jacket as a makeshift hang glider. Feer only just managed to grab onto one of his legs before it was too late, and he was yanked up as well. As they were whipped away by the wind, seemingly as light as a feather, the astounded onlookers were bombarded by cackles and jibes from the two, only interrupted by an argument over who should be the one to hold onto the jacket.

"Ha ha! You won't be so lucky next time, Pete, we will all come for you, just you wait."

Soon, though, they were out of sight, blown away by the heavy winds and obscured by the dark grey clouds. The passengers on the boat all breathed a collective sigh of relief as if they had all just simultaneously gotten over a nasty illness. Reggie immediately stopped vomiting and just seemed a little tired from the ordeal.

Chapter 10
A Hero and a Curse

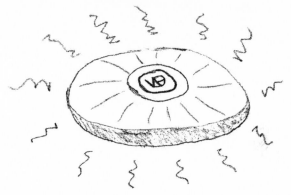

With the demons out of sight, Brigid began to apologetically free the creatures from her net. The two small twin brothers shared the older girl's red hair and freckles, they were too young to understand how dangerous their playtime interruption was and quickly resumed smiling. Once they had stopped shivering in terror, the Wikings came to humbly apologise, one of the twins even took an adventurous tug at their beards. Soon enough the two little ones had found perches on the shoulders of their huge would-be captors and were giggling, perching their seal-like bodies on the backs of their captors-turned-playmates. Meanwhile, the older one sat and explained things to Brigid and Pete.

"Thank you so much, it seems it wasn't enough for that doctor to place a curse on us. They also had to trick people into hunting us as well. My name is Elkie, and these are my little brothers: Harald and Thor."

"Curse you?" asked Pete.

"We used to be Viking people as well. We would sail around the seas like all the other Vikings, but then Feer and Diztruzt came and cursed everyone in our village. Soon people started seeing us as scary creatures from the sea, all the while those two would be nearby, laughing as if it was all a cruel joke to them. With time, not only were we perceived as sea creatures but we then slowly began to turn into exactly those creatures and had to leave the land, we have been swimming around avoiding hunters who used to be our friends ever since. I'm surprised you saw us as harmless, Pete. You seemed to be the only one able to see through the nastiness and duplicity of Feer and Diztruzt. You really have done something heroic today, Pete."

"You don´t look at all monstrous to me, just a bit like a human seal," said Pete, intrigued by their curse and secretly flush with pride at being called heroic.

"They have changed the way they looked," said Brigid. "When I first laid eyes upon them, they had sharp scales and vicious claws and evil faces... and now, they don't appear to look like that at all. We were tricked into thinking they were evil. I only just remembered the village that disappeared once those two evildoers had flown off." Brigid spoke slowly and sadly, ashamed of herself and angry with the demons. She was still baffled that they had all been so badly tricked. Not only had they somehow lost partial control of their minds and memories but had even been made to see things that were simply not true. She quickly shook this off, and her resolve returned, and she picked her shoulders up, never one to dwell on the past and things she could not change.

"How can we lift this curse, my fellows? We all knew people from your village, what about your older sister? Margaret and I were good friends, I remember now. We will do anything we can to help," she said. Her voice once again in its natural booming tone, now she had rediscovered a purpose. The others all nodded their agreement, solemnly pledging to help their lost friends.

"Margaret explained it to us, I'm afraid you can only completely lift the curse by stopping the demons," said Elkie the seal. "The demons are coming from beyond the Time Line. No one can get there, we've tried. My older sister went looking and we haven't seen her since," she stifled a tear saying this.

"We have to help. We have to make up for all the distress we have caused you! And for being so stupid that we allowed such evil characters to influence us. We will set sail for the station immediately," Brigid said, promptly standing up yelling commands to take action.

"Turn around you slow sailors, I've seen slugs row faster than you! Heave Ho!"

The industrious seamanship of the Wikings had returned and The Whooping Wanderer was sailing back to the platform. Elkie and her brothers were already completely ignored by the Wikings as they turned to their tasks at hand.

Elkie turned to Pete. "Thanks for everything. Those Wikings are good people, but I don't think they can help.

They are one with their ship and therefore could not travel without it, and they can't fit the whole thing on the carriages of the Time Line."

"Don´t worry, maybe the Wikings cannot help just yet, but I'm sure they will find a way. My friends and I will definitely help you! I´m stuck here in this world, anyway, so why not do some good whilst I am here. I´ll find the demons and lift your curse," Pete said, without really knowing where his sudden bravery had come from. Demons did sound like a fairly scary and unpleasant group after all, especially if Feer and Diztruzt were anything to go by. And that was just dealing with two of them. What would happen if there were many more demons? He had just finished his sentence and the onset of his doubts came, when Reggie chipped in from next to him, always seeming to know when he needed support.

"We are with you, Peter, we shall help find the demons."

"Definitely! For what an intriguing proposal this is turning out to be; beyond the Time Line… My, why what an adventure this is shaping up to be, is it not?" Phil finally butted in, having been strangely and unusually silent for a while, rummaging the ship and staring at the clouds where the demons disappeared, searching for clues while they spoke.

"Oh, thank you! Really, but I can't ask you to do this." Elkie was nearly moved to tears by this display of support.

"No need to thank us. We're going on an adventure, we want to help you, for we hope to be the greatest searchers and discoverers and we will find the demons and undo all the bad and evil things they've done," Phil replied with mock grandeur and a bow, that perhaps did echo some deeper heroics that had stirred within him.

"Besides, no way to go but forward and I have a feeling this might help you get back to your world, Pete. Interesting that only you saw through the demonic curse, hmm… yes, most intriguing." He pulled a tattered notepad from his colourful patchwork robe, jotting things down with a quick, scribbling hand.

The longship very soon made it back to the station, which still looked strange jutting out from the sea, with rails that led directly into the depths of beyond. Brigid and her Wikings were determined to sail on as quickly as possible after depositing Peter and his friends, so they could search the seas for the demons. They could not get The Whooping Wanderer on the train, and it was as much a member of the crew as the rest. Despite that, the farewells between the Wikings and the Elkie and her two little siblings, as well as Pete and his companions, was heartfelt. It was definitely as if they had made friends for life. Even though their time together had been so brief.

As the trio stepped off the ship and back onto the solid platform, Reggie's colouring noticeably improved, although his stomach was still making odd noises. Elkie splashed back into the water, but just before diving under with her brothers, she uttered another "Thank you" and asked them to wait there for something. With that, she sped off under the sea, with a speed that would rival a torpedo. For about two minutes the group stood expectantly, watching the waves where she'd been. Whilst waiting,

Reggie patted Pete on the back (as best he good with his claws).

"You should be proud of yourself today."

Pete looked back and thanked him with a nod, lost in thought.

Soon enough, Elkie returned, carrying a small black token. Poking her head out of the water, arms outstretched, she passed it up to Pete.

"This is what Feer and Diztruzt used to curse us. It's a demon stone. It buzzed whenever they were around. Maybe you could use it to try to find them?"

Pete took the token, it felt unpleasant in his hands, so he quickly tucked it away in a pocket and thanked Elkie.

"No, please don't thank me. Thank you, you were a real hero today. I'll be telling everyone about it and your kind offer to help lift our curse. Good luck," she answered, before diving off into the ocean once again, chasing her brothers.

As they walked back to the train, the storm cleared up, revealing a beautiful sunset. The red of the sun licked across the strings of clouds, creating an illusory fire that matched Pete's newfound purpose and pride from today's events.

Chapter 11
The Next Step

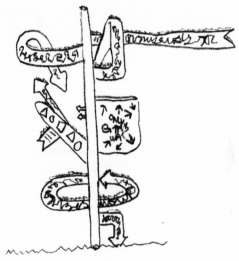

As they re-entered the Time Line once more, Pete's mind was rushing so fast with thoughts of his heroic new goal and the places he'd been and people he'd met, that he was hard-pressed to imagine the boredom that had got him here in the first place. As the train departed and sank once more beneath the waves, the deep blue hue that wrapped around the carriage calmed him and made his exhaustion very palpable. Pete fell into a deep sleep, almost as soon as they sat down. Reggie and Phil were discussing interesting places to visit, and how they were going to help Elkie and the cursed village, whilst also sharing their experiences of a particular Corsican restaurant they had both been to.

Unaware of Pete's sudden unconsciousness, they turned to him, asking if he had any plans where to go next. On seeing him resting, they chuckled to each other, letting him sleep and continuing their discussions of fine Corsican cuisine.

Some time passed, and their conversation had moved on to Olmec culture and whether they found, them, or their successors, the Mayans, more hospitable to guests and such other very important topics. Meanwhile, Pete had slowly sunk into the seat, now almost horizontal, leaning on Reggie's tail. He was peacefully sleeping a dreamless sleep when suddenly he felt a phone ringing in his pocket. Clawing himself awake, he was reacquainted with the absurdity of his situation, seeing Phil engaged in a heated discussion with Reggie, three bears, and another dinosaur about the quality of seafood and how it had changed over time.

"Why Philosophocles, it's obvious there is less oxygen in the water now than there used to be, the fish were simply bigger and tastier back then."

"Nonsense, the fish were as likely to eat you as feed you back then, and there is no better fish than a good Athenian Tuna," retorted Phil, the three bears behind him nodding in agreement.

"Ah look, Pete's woken up," Reggie said, and they turned to him, but not without exchanging looks that said their discussion would continue.

Pete clawed for the ringing phone, instead of finding a phone, however, upon reaching into his pockets, he pulled out the token that Elkie had given him. It was humming and vibrating quite fiercely, enough that Pete had to grip it, so it didn't wiggle out of his hand. He held it out with a meaningful glance at Reggie and Phil. Both immediately understood the significance of the ringing token and began collecting their things to disembark at the next stop. It must mean that there were demons close by.

Their fellow onlookers exchanged confused glances at the immediate stop in the interesting discussion. Then they dispersed to find new seats, each feeling satisfied that they had won the argument and not really interested in the strange token, these three mismatched travellers, or their mission. The train began to slow down, but on the long list of stops, this one was only marked with a series of edgeless squiggles.

"They must be here then," Pete said, with a nervous feeling, for while Feer and Diztruzt had not seemed overtly dangerous, he had a distinct sense that they were a lot more powerful and evil than they appeared, to be able to trick Big Brigid and curse an entire village.

"How will we find them and how do we know this is the right place to get off?" said Reggie, just as they stepped off the train.

"And where are we? None of the signs make any sense," said Phil.

The answers to these questions would prove harder than they thought, as they felt lost almost immediately after leaving the train. They were greeted by the most topsy-turvy impostor of a city any of them had ever experienced. There were no hard edges anywhere, and the roads and buildings all seemed to curve and meander further, merging into the city. It was very hard to tell where one object began and another ended. The people they saw looked just as confused as they felt. Pete saw the same man three times within a very short period, each time after being sure he had just seen him walk off down another street. Even the signs proved no help, as the letters were all jumbled into shapes that looked like no alphabet Pete recognised, or even as if they belonged to any language at all, come to think of it. Even the biggest, grandest sign, which was the first thing they saw as they got off the train, was barely legible and welcomed them to a place none of them had heard about.

"What on earth do you think has happened here?" said Phil.

"Well, I suppose it certainly seems the demons we have been looking for have had a hand in this mess," Reggie wondered, examining the abstract representation of what a city might look like if logic had gone on holiday.

"Well, let's start looking, we won't find out if we stay standing here," Pete said, still shocking himself with his newfound confidence. He strode off with a very determined step into the impossible streets, not really waiting for the others to follow him but trusting that they would.

Chapter 12
Impossibul

Finding their way anywhere proved very tough. The streets were twisted and wound back on themselves, so much so that when Pete tried visualising a top-down view of where they had walked, he was almost sure they had been going backwards, without re-crossing any of their paths. The locals seemed no better off. Most seemed just as lost and confused as them and anyone who strode with purpose was soon revealed to be just as lost. Anyone they approached for directions looked at them oddly, and then answered with a shrug, almost as if to say: "What a silly thing to ask for." Sometimes, they would be following behind someone and momentarily lose sight of them, just for them to reappear walking towards them. They must have spotted the same turn, where they saw the same store owner five times, he was pacing around lamenting that he had lost his shop and asking if anyone had seen it. Altogether, the lack of straight edges anywhere was incredibly baffling, everything seemed to be wiggly and wonky.

The whole city seemed confused. Buildings were standing on awkward foundations that did not support them; steep slippery ramps were in the places where stairs should have been, leaving many trapped in the upper stories of buildings, no one able to enter or exit. Everything was sloped or rounded, so much that even finding a solid footing was difficult. People were slipping and falling and meandering in an odd, dejected panic, that never fully manifested itself due to their intense confusion. Everything was chaos. They passed a fruit market where mountains of apples were rolling around, crushing carts and knocking people over. Pete and Phil had been solidly staring at the ground, hoping to stay stable and stepping very carefully to avoid falling over. They began to get very tired with this endless wandering around and not getting anywhere. However, Reggie's clawed feet made the uneven ground trivial, and he watched everyone around him stumbling with a mixture of amusement and worry.

"We're never going to get anywhere, and no one can help, and this token has been buzzing for hours, and we are no closer to finding the demons," Pete uttered, all in one despairing sentence. They all sat down to rest, and Pete pulled out the token from his pocket angrily.

"I just wanted to finally help someone and lift the curse on those poor villagers stuck in the ocean. Now I'm entirely lost, and I've brought you two with me into this misadventure and chaos," he said apologetically, feeling guilty how his foolish exuberance had led to him charging off into the winding streets without any real plan. Phil and Reggie looked at one another, unsure of what to say.

"Adventure! Remember, that's why I'm here and let me tell you coming with you has given me plenty more new experiences than sitting back in my cosy room in the Acropolis. Whatever happens, I'm glad I came with you," Phil said awkwardly, unused to comforting people, or even noticing when people needed comforting.

"And I would still be sat in my chair at home, complaining about my creaking bones and meeting an incredibly dull old Allosaurus couple for tea if I had not met you. There's no need to apologise, I should be thanking you." Reggie spoke reassuringly and Phil nodded in agreement. Pete looked back at them gratefully and sniffled a bit.

"Thanks, you two, for everything... But even when I try, I can never do anything properly," he said despondently. "I just gave Elkie and her people false hope. Saving them is just too hard," he continued, kicking the ground in frustration.

Just then, they heard a voice behind them, it came from a tall man wearing a turban and flowing orange silk robes, who had been standing near them and eavesdropping on their conversation.

"Well, if it were easy then it can't be that good then, or worth doing. Doing good things in life has to be hard sometimes, or everyone would be doing them and then they would not be all that good any more, would they?"

the stranger said.

They all turned to face him in unison. He smiled absentmindedly, as if unaware of their predicament and that they did not yet know who he was.

"Who are you?" Reggie said, still taken aback by the interruption.

"Why I am the renowned explorer, adventurer and solver of hard problems. My name is Muhammed Ibrahim Battuta. It seems we have a similar goal. You see, I travelled here with the permission of a Great Khan, along with Princess Bayala, who is returning to her city. The city of... well what we thought was Constantinople, now it seems it has changed its name to Impossibul? Meanwhile, it has become a right jumble, she says it looks nothing like the Constantinople she remembers growing up. As you can see, this place is in no state for my princess to return to. She came to stay with her father as she prepares to have her baby, so it's all a rather bad time for such a mess. I am famed for my sense of direction but even so, I get lost here, and no amount of explorer's intuition helps in this meaningless tangle. All the angles are gone from the city. It is really as if someone has taken all the corners out of everything in this city, leaving only "S" shapes behind. I cannot think of any reason someone would do this, other than to cause stress and chaos. I suspect the work of someone, or something supernaturally devious."

"So I've set Bayala down in a field outside the city, while I try to scout things out. It was my intention to only be gone for a short while, as I did not anticipate that the problem would be as bad as it now seems to be. I probably should not be gone too long, she does not like waiting."

Pete looked up from his throes of self-doubt and curiously eyed the fast-talking man in the turban, thinking hard over what Ibrahim had just said.

"Do you know what's wrong with this place?" he asked determinedly, clearing up the last traces of his sobbing.

"Why yes, it's as I said. All the angles are gone, and my if it isn't making sightseeing a massive pain in this city," Ibn Battuta answered matter-of-factly.

"But where did they go?" Pete was getting a little frustrated with his seeming reluctance to explain the knowledge he had of the situation clearly, or maybe he was more annoyed with himself not really understanding the man's answer.

"Oh, I have no clue, that's what I'm trying to find out," said Muhammed Ibrahim Battuta.

All of a sudden, with a quick look at the endlessly winding (but never straight) roads around him Pete understood what this stranger in the orange silk robes was telling them. Although Pete was back to square one on finding a solution, without any further knowledge. Finally, at least he knew what the problem was. In fact, the more he thought about it, the more ridiculous it seemed. How could angles just go missing from a city? What kind of new nonsense was this, angles don't just disappear, do they? But then again, so far it was not as if anything in Outermind really could be measured up against his understanding of his world back home with all its logic.

Pete had a sudden thought, an idea that certainly would not work in his world but... What if... surely... no...

maybe… yes… and then he looked around him and asked Muhammed Ibrahim Battuta, "Do you have something to write with?"

Ibrahim looked back at Pete as if it were a perfectly normal request for the situation.

"Why of course. I always have chalk with me. It's right here in my pocket. I can make plans anywhere you know, draw maps, all that." He continued to list the many virtues of always carrying a piece of chalk, as he passed Pete a grey-white stick from a pocket within his flowing robes. Pete immediately got to work and drew a perfectly normal "L" shape on the ground between the group.

 As they stood there around this "L" that Pete had so spontaneously drawn, he looked up with a proud beam on his face. Then he saw his onlookers wore confused expressions. So far, none of the others had understood what he was doing. His pride immediately felt very silly as he stood up, faced with a regular, everyday, run-of-the-mill L-shape, drawn in chalk on the ground before him. Phil and Reggie looked at him expectantly as if he had started an unfinished map or plan of some sort, they were waiting for further explanation. Clearly, they were still none the wiser. Ibrahim, however, was scratching his beard and nodding sagely. They stood there for another minute or so, even though it felt like an age of embarrassment to Pete before he finally said, "Err, sorry, that was it. I thought it was a good idea."

Just as he was blushing and beginning to feel useless

and lost again, the "L" he had drawn leapt up with a zip and a pop, and before any of them could react, it shot upwards with a ping. It was as if the chalky "L" had been pulled by some great magnet, so fast that it left a jet stream tracing where it flew. They barely had time to look up, just seeing it soaring off until it shot up through the clouds.

"Well, I must say that was unexpected, never knew chalk could fly," Phil spoke, already reaching down to investigate where the "L" had been.

"You absolute GENIUS!" Ibrahim shouted at Pete, clapping his hands down onto his shoulders in a congratulatory manner.

"Come with me, all of you." And then he bounded off towards the outskirts of the city. (Or at least what could be the outskirts, judging by the buildings getting smaller. Really it could have been anywhere, no one could make heads or tails of that, as the city was still very much disorganised in a snaking jumble.)

Pete was still staring up at the sky where his "L" had gone, while Phil scrabbled for any trace of the chalk where Pete had drawn it onto the cobblestones. Reggie stood between them in befuddlement, his long snout alternated between looking up at the sky, the ground and the fleeing orange figure. He still did not understand what was happening.

Reggie then tapped the other two on the shoulder, bringing them out of their distraction, saying, "I think we should decide soon whether or not we should follow him before he disappears. It does not look like Muhammed Ibrahim Battuta is waiting for us."

No decision-making was needed, as both Pete and Phil started running after Ibrahim once they realised the speed at which he was leaving.

"Oh, well, I suppose we are going after him then," Reggie said to nobody. He sighed as he hunched over into a running stance to catch up.

Chapter 13
Angels, or Are They Angles?

They sprinted through the winding streets of Impossibul, chasing after Muhammed Ibrahim Battuta. All three of them were rather short, so they relied on Reggie, who would occasionally leap above the crowd on his piston-like legs to point the way. Finally, they arrived at a field where Ibrahim was now standing in a revelatory pose as if announcing the next act at a circus. His expectation of their reactions was justified; right beside the proudly beaming orange-clad man stood a sparkling new 20th-century helicopter. It was parked nonchalantly in the middle of a field, surrounded by horse-drawn carts and a few unfazed oxen.

Reggie jumped in fright, turning to tell Pete that this was the mysterious vehicle which had terrified him with turbulence, long ago when he had flown with the pterodactyls.

"Well, Pete, let's see where your drawing went." He still spoke theatrically, obviously pleased with his flying contraption. He stepped into the cockpit, wriggling his fingers, ready at the controls. The others stepped into the passenger seats tentatively, as if it could vanish at any moment.

"Where did you get a helicopter?" Pete inquired, not sure if he would get a straight answer.

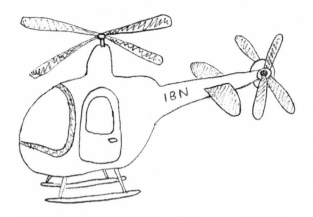

"Why, it's a gift from a fellow explorer living in the 1970s. He's a very wealthy man who had apparently gotten tired of listening to me complain about travelling sores from horses, camels and elephants, so he gave me this." This was all said as if it made perfect chronological sense, the flow of time in this world took some getting used to for Pete. He continued speaking, describing the wonderful convenience that flight had over traditional old-fashioned travel, but what he said was mostly lost over the spinning of the blades as the engine started up. Pete had certainly never been in a helicopter before, and neither Phil nor Reggie had been more than a jump's height off the ground before, (except Reggie's one brief Pterodactyl mishap in his distant youth). Reggie and Phil's faces contorted in terror and amazement respectively as the ground suddenly began to move away beneath them. Since normal conversation was impossible over the roar of the helicopter's engine, (unfortunate as none of them had questioned Ibrahim about where they were going, being too absorbed with the surprise of the helicopter) they instead all began looking out the windows, trying to gain a view of the impossible city from the air. Except for Phil, who was looking up at the blades and furiously scribbling notes on a papyrus pad. Pete glanced over at the page, seeing he had titled his notes: "How does flying spinny thing work???" He shook his head, wondering for not the first time, whether Phil was indeed a genius or a madman. Momentarily forgetting that Phil did belong to another time and that in this instance Pete had the advantage of coming from an age where helicopters and aeroplanes had been invented and aeronautical knowledge was available in science textbooks.

Suddenly they were above the clouds. They expected a bit of searching followed by trial and error to discover the missing angles from the city below. They certainly did not imagine their find would be so glaringly obvious, awaiting right on the other side of the clouds, and so very near. Around them; jumping, hollering, tripping and falling, were all the missing angles of the city below, street corners floated solidly between signs, words and various edged objects of all sorts, everything that seemed missing from the city below.

"Oi," Pete yelled out the side, cupping his hands to his mouth in order to make the sound carry over the noise of the helicopter. The angles ignored him, carrying on as they had, with slight detours to avoid the hovering machine. Pete felt the token Elkie had given him buzzing even stronger than it had earlier and peered into the blue sky with worry. Off in the distance, just visible between all the bits and pieces haphazardly floating around, he saw a dark bulbous mass moving towards them. A bit of a way behind the mass, as if it was a sullying influence, came the most beautiful creature Pete had ever seen.

Both approached the helicopter. The dark blob, that had looked like one shape from a distance, was in fact constantly altering its form, but basically looked like an ever-changing combination of all the pencil doodles Pete had drawn in class when he was not paying attention. Needless to say, Pete was not much good at drawing. Despite this amorphous oddity, it only held their attention briefly, as what came behind was such a stunning, enrapturing sight that they lost all interest in anything else. It looked vaguely like a person, but it was at least twice the size of even "Big" Brigid Birgitteson, who lived up to her namesake of being the largest human Pete had ever seen. Everything about this marvellous being was reminiscent of precious metals: golden hair, bronzed skin, silver clothing. It shone so much that it almost hurt to look at, but they could not pull their eyes away from it. In a mysterious, otherworldly and inhuman way, it was the most beautiful being any of the passengers had ever seen. It seemed to be looking at them all at once, each passenger felt it stare them directly in the eye with a gaze so piercing and terrible, yet kind and benevolent, that if they could bring themselves to avert their eyes from its glory, they would, just to save any possible embarrassment in front of this glorious god.

"Angels," the godlike being spoke this one word, but it carried all the weight of a full speech. Its voice was paradoxically soft and understanding, but hard and forceful at the same time. Despite paying no attention to the shouts from the helicopter, the angles dancing about the clouds all snapped to attention, silently "facing" the two creatures as if they were in reverent prayer.

As they all looked, they became transfixed, unable to avert their eyes from the beautiful divinity of it all. When the being commanded the debris around it, its word became law. The "angles", edged bits and pieces of the city below, slowly transformed into a majestic sea of glowing "angels" with fluffy, feathered wings.

"Greetings, walkers of the earth below," the glowing figure finally said, after a long, awestruck silence. Leaning precariously out of the helicopter to get as close as possible, the group responded with a chorus of stammered hellos and waves.

"What are you doing here, little ones?" To that, none of them could respond. Their task seemed like a distant afterthought and none of them quite remembered why they were here. Seeing their silence, the creature smiled reassuringly. Then, for a barely noticeable split second, the smile turned to an evil smirk, as if it was getting a mischievous idea, but once again it spoke serenely:

"No matter, my friends, take my hand and join us, we can all be angels, you know."

It approached the helicopter, and they all jostled for position, reaching out towards the figure, hoping to be the first to take the hand of this wonderful creature.

Ibrahim was in the cockpit and was, therefore, the closest. Leaving the controls, he stood pressed up against the wall, both hands outside the window. Just as he was about to make contact with the outstretched, too-perfect hand… they plummeted, going into a sickening spin, as the rotors chopped haplessly at the air. Without Muhammed Ibrahim Battuta's capable hands on the controls, this marvel of 20th-century engineering became a downwardly spinning meteor of steel. By some miracle, everyone inside managed to retract their hands and grab onto something quickly enough to avoid being thrown out of the side of the helicopter.

For a while, everything became a blur of sky and clouds rushing past them. Not that the passengers would have noticed, being too busy screaming and hanging on for dear life. Pete looked into the front where he saw Ibrahim was not joining in on their panic. Instead, he was stroking his long beard in ponderous thought. Pete banged on the window separating them, and all Ibrahim did was to turn around smiling. He held up his hand with five fingers outstretched, counting them down painstakingly slowly. Pete looked at him as if he was mad. We're all going to crash because of this strange man, he thought. Ibrahim just looked back at them calmly, as now all three of them were wildly banging on the glass. Phil pointed at the controls hoping it would help jog his memory. Only when his finger-countdown reached zero did he finally turn around, grasping the controls. After some struggle and strange noises from the rotors, Ibrahim righted the helicopter and they were once again hovering, now far below the clouds, leaving the figures above with the angles/angels, or whatever they were, feeling like their stomachs had also remained several thousand metres above them.

By now they were scarily close to the ground, but the rest of their descent was controlled and comfortable. They stepped off the helicopter, after what seemed a lifetime but was only a few minutes. Feeling shocked and dazed, they were very grateful for the presence of solid ground and felt lucky to still be alive. Ibrahim stepped out of the front of the helicopter.

"Well, don't get too used to being on land yet, we're going back up there," he said.

The other three turned to face him with various incredulous expressions. Surely, they had misheard? They had barely survived the first flight and yet they were being asked to go back up? Pete's immediate reaction was anger. Reggie looked terrified, and Phil looked confused for the first time; a strange expression for him, as he was usually the one causing the confusion. This plummet must have thrown him very off-kilter indeed for him to act like this.

"What do you think you were doing?!" yelled Pete. "You're crazy!"

"I... I... I do not believe going b... b... back up there is an altogether grand p... p... plan," Reggie stammered.

"Wha, huh, what's going on?" Phil said to no one in particular, spinning his whole body to look up at the sky, then to Ibrahim, then to the helicopter, as if unsure which issue to tackle first.

Ibrahim looked at all three of them knowingly and announced that there was a reason he had acted the way he had. He thought he might have figured out what was going on; both up in the air and also with the city. At the promise of answers, they all stopped talking and shouting, leaving an expectant silence over the group.

Just as the silence was about to go on long enough that the tirade of questions would restart; Ibrahim Battuta spoke, as if only just realising he had promised that he would explain:

"I have travelled far and wide and heard some interesting stories lately. I think I know who those two beings up in the sky are. Foul creatures! Demons, even, some say. Though you wouldn't know from this particular pair, as they have disguised themselves quite amazingly. They are called Kaoz and Dezeptchen, masters of trickery. One of them is the dark bulbous mass, the other, the alluring creature. I do not know all that much about them, but I do think the plummet that I orchestrated was far better than the alternative! Had we stayed up there with them, we would have been beholden to the whims of the stunningly beautiful Dezeptchen or absorbed into the madness of Kaoz, the dark blob behind. You should be congratulating me on my amazing actions rather than being angry."

It took a little while for things to fit into place, but the others finally understood what had just happened, even though it all seemed a jumble in their minds, which were still getting over Dezeptchen's spellbound allure.

They had once again come across demons, even though they looked nothing alike, something about them reminded Pete of Dr Feer and Distruzt. Once again, the demons had used cunningly clever disguises to stop them from being discovered and letting them continue to wreak havoc with the denizens of Outermind. Pete pouted in frustration; he should have paid more attention. The demon that Ibrahim called Dezeptchen had distracted him from the buzzing stone and all the other signs that something was not right.

Chapter 14
Skydiving Around the Problem

Pete was eager to return and face his foe – now that he knew who and what that foe was. Not only that, it seemed that they had inadvertently stumbled upon where the demons were. Better yet, it might bring them one step closer to being able to help Elkie's cursed village. Meanwhile, Muhammed Ibrahim Battuta must have been more shaken than he seemed, because he raised a cautioning hand before Pete stepped back onto the helicopter.

"Pete wait, I would like nothing more than to give those two their comeuppance; as a navigator, I find this sort of directional commotion to be an absolute travesty. We have to be careful though, if we go up there again now, we will just be transfixed by the demons in the same way we were before. We need to have a plan."

"What do we do then? What is the plan?" Pete said impatiently. Ibn Battuta pulled out the stick of chalk Pete had used to draw his absent "L".

"The plan is that we draw a plan of course," he said, starting to scribble on a stone beneath them. "Let's see now… Kaoz and Dezeptchen here, big NO for now." He drew as he spoke; a big cloud with a hasty sketch of the demons was crossed out, then a downward spiral to indicate their descent. Some distance away, he drew the Time Line station, with a lot of question marks in between their current position and it. Stopping for a moment, putting the chalk in his mouth as he thought, he made a "eureka" gesture, holding the white stick high in the air, before frantically drawing and writing haphazardly on the rocks. When he was finished, his plan seemed incredibly convoluted, with arrows drawn going every which way and squiggly drawings, which obscured seemingly important writing and vice versa.

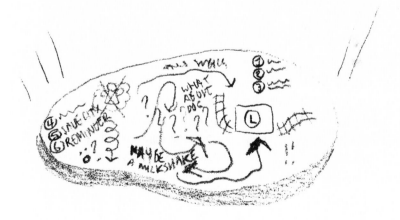

Pete gave up trying to take in the bigger picture and just focused on what seemed logical. There was a numbered "list" off to one side of the drawing that sort of explained things (if you looked very carefully).

1. Goggles!!! Help us not see and be tricked

2. Victorian England (this was surrounded by a circle with an arrow pointing to it that said "special eyewear goggle-maker here")

3. Skydive around confusion to Time Line (this had an arrow placing it in between 1 and 2)

4. Sort out Kaoz and Dezeptchen (the demons in the sky with the angles)

5. Save city

6. Reminder: Princess Bayala having child, remember to congratulate!

7. Uh oh… Princess Bayala, probably wondering where I've been

As he wrote the last number on the list, Ibrahim panicked, looking around as if expecting his heavily pregnant patron to be stalking the topsy-turvy city looking for him, to give him an earful. He quickly implored the others that they had to get on with the plan right here and now, as he had to get back to his princess as soon as possible. The others had not even seen him this worried when he stepped out of the nearly crash-landed helicopter. Nor did he seem worried about the demons. His princess was obviously a hard taskmaster! He told them to get back in the helicopter and he would take them back to the Time Line, all the while mumbling and practising excuses to himself, in preparation for his return to the princess.

"Sorry I'm back late, I was trying to... Oh sorry, madam, I was sick. No, no... What, missing, me? Can't be, I was here the whole time, tending to the horses."

Pete grinned as they walked past the distraught Ibrahim, tentatively retaking their places in the helicopter; this Princess Bayala sounded fierce, he thought. As they took off and began flying over the city, they heard faint yells from the cockpit, the rotor blades interrupting the words, which sounded like someone shouting in the distance. Ibrahim was once again giving them instructions.

"Under your seats! Put on the backpacks! Remember; go to Victorian England. I can't join you. I need to get back to the princess! You will need to find the goggles, look for inventors in Victorian England, I heard one of them has developed demon-proof glass. Come back once you have them so that we can conquer the demons."

The others scrabbled around under their seats, following the instructions.

If it was possible to yell in a hurry, that's what Ibrahim now did: "Quick! Those are parachutes, pull the cord at the top of the right strap, you'll probably be fine. Okay ready. 5, 4, never mind, JUMP!"

As expected, none of them jumped, not even Phil, who was the one person here who might; the thrill of adventure being a large part of his decision to embark on this whole journey. They had had no training. They were just not prepared for this. It was all happening way too fast. And to just simply jump out of a helicopter when someone they had only known for such a short time suggested it, seemed too overwhelming and just not something they didn't imagine going horribly wrong.

Pete could see the Time Line station passing below, a beacon of solidity amidst the ever-shifting streets around it. If they missed the station, they would never find their way back to it on foot. He made an instant decision. Taking a very, very deep breath, he took Phil's hand and Reggie's claw... Then he exhaled, took another very, very deep breath, decided to trust Ibrahim and jumped.

Seconds turned to minutes, which turned to hours and then back to seconds again. By the time they had all gotten over the panic and exhilaration of freefall, they had a brief moment of peace, when the air resistance had caught up with them. It almost did not feel like they were falling. Reggie lost his nerve first, letting go of their hands and clawing at his parachute to unfold it, he zoomed off above them once he had managed to pull the string and the parachute unfolded, while they continued their downward motion. The ground still looked quite far away but seeing as his parachute training had consisted solely of a few minutes listening to Ibrahim's barely audible yelling, Pete thought it was a good idea to get some practice, before having to land. He pulled the zip as well, making his parachute unfold just like Reggie's, leaving Phil, who had been shouting exuberantly the whole way, diving continuously further down below them. No longer rushing towards the ground, Pete now looked below him in a more peaceful mindset, once he had gotten some grasp on how the parachute worked. He still worried about Phil, though. Phil had positioned himself into a nosedive.

"YAHOOOO!" His adrenaline-fuelled whoops trailed off as he fell. Just as Pete was about to truly worry about

Phil and his lack of judgement and understanding of the severity of the situation, he saw Phil's bright yellow parachute pop out below him, like a firework against the urban background. Thank goodness, Phil was a little bit sensible after all.

Pete could now make out more details below him in the landscape, and that they were nearing the station. And in fact, he could now see that there was a train at the station. The train that had stopped at the station was closing its doors, and the signals changed, indicating it was about to leave. As Pete got close, he saw that Phil had landed on top of the train. "Quick, it's about to leave, this is the only way we'll make it," Phil shouted upwards. Despite it being his first parachute flight and Phil's rushing, Pete landed fairly gracefully, considering the circumstances. Phil had been waiting for some time, storing his pent-up excitement for someone to share it with. The two friends enthusiastically discussed their drop, with no regard for all the strange looks people were giving to these two mysterious figures who had swooped out of the sky and were now jumping up and down on top of the train, exuberantly exclaiming at each other.

"WOW! Oh, that was incredible. I may be sick. But who cares that was incredible!" Pete said, jumping from foot to foot. "I want to do that again."

"Well, that's another reason to find those goggles. That Ibrahim fellow might let us go for another round when all this is fixed," Phil answered, looking up at the helicopter fading into the distance.

Their joy was soon dashed when they realised Reggie

had pulled his parachute too early. He was dangling awkwardly from the cords of his parachute, its design more suited to human-shaped creatures. Though Reggie tried to steer into more of a dive, he was not making as fast headway as the other two would have liked. All they could do was stare, willing Reggie to move faster through the air so he would catch up with them. The train started to move, and Reggie grasped the air wildly with swinging claws, trying to pull himself closer by pushing the air behind him. Pete and Phil ran along the roof of the train as it sped up, keeping pace with Reggie, but it was no use. The last carriage was just out of reach when Reggie got to train-height, and they all looked at each other, shocked and agape. It definitely looked as if Reggie would be left behind. Pete and Phil were just out of reach, and their hands floundered uselessly for the dinosaur's tail.

This simply could not be! Reggie had to come along. After all, they were all in this together.

Suddenly, a figure popped out from what looked like a small canvas tent on top of the train that they had not noticed during their approach. The figure reached out with an umbrella, using its handle to tug Reggie in. She almost got dragged off with him, pulled by the resistance of the parachute against the speed of the train, but Pete and Phil helped brace her. For a moment, there was a struggle as Reggie panicked, trying to remove the parachute that was poorly designed for raptor arms, and not intended to be taken off in a hurry. Finally, it slipped off, whooshing backwards, while Reggie crashed on top of them in a pile. He had made it!!! Thank goodness.

Chapter 15
Margaret, the Forgotten Roof Riders
and Breakneck Speeds.

Before they had even managed to untangle themselves from the pile-up, the small woman who had saved Reggie started yelling.

"You can see me, you can see me!" She was hard to make out, the only way Pete could describe her appearance was "fuzzy".

Pete got up first, while Reggie and Phil had to untangle tail from beard. He looked around and noticed that there were more of these previously unnoticed tents and all sorts of creatures getting out from them. Both the tents and their residents all shared the fuzzy look of the woman who helped me. The selection was as varied as it was inside the train carriages below, except they all looked slightly immaterial and intangible as if they were only halfway present.

"Here, gather round. I think the strangers can see us," the small woman said. The figures all half-drifted, half-walked, towards them. They now all stood in a semicircle at the back of the train, looking expectantly upon the new arrivals. Pete simply stared back, still rattled. Once again here was something that simply did not make sense, a whole fuzzy ghostlike menagerie living on top of a train. Would it never stop? New things kept popping up that were almost beyond imagination, surely there could not be that many surprises left? The figures led by the small woman started advancing on the small group, almost hungrily it seemed.

Should they be worried? It started to seem so. There were so many of these ethereal beings, which got Pete thinking too much about old ghost stories.

In the meantime, the train had been picking up speed and by this point had started to go faster than Pete thought trains could even possibly go, the speed was a lot more noticeable on the roof instead of the carriage. Every few seconds he felt another whoosh, as the train accelerated even more. Quickly, the whooshes turned to the ear-popping bangs of sonic booms as the train broke the sound barrier. Pete looked back at the advancing crowd and felt his eyes start to well up and his hair whipping around on his face. Another bang and now the surrounding "countryside?" was an incomprehensible blur that seemed to be breaking the rules of how much could fit into his view. He saw whole cities, so clear that he could pick out street signs, but they were distant spots in the horizon. Blue, yellow and pink started streaking across his vision, like little bolts of horizontal lightning. Soon they were going so fast that even the air around them became painful. He started to feel his body siphoning off into the infinity behind him, his cheeks were being pulled back and his skin seemed to be melting into a liquid. Shots of pain ran up and down him and he just managed to open his mouth a little to whimper.

"Help..."

The last he heard before everything went black was, "You're right, they can see us."

When Pete and his friends next came to, they were inside a very dull coloured room, with brown-grey canvased walls and a metallic floor. Pete looked wildly at his friends and saw the same terrified look in their eyes as they saw in his.

"Sorry, we are awfully sorry, we forgot you aren't so used to being outside at warp speed."

All around them were the incorporeal ghosts that they had seen earlier.

"Where are we? Who are you?" Phil stammered as he came to his senses.

The female ghost, who looked like the one who saved them earlier, although it was hard to tell as they all kept phasing in and out, introduced herself and said, "I am Margaret, or at least I call myself that. We are 'The Forgotten'. As the warp speed increased, you all blacked out, and we rushed out to bring you inside our tents. The speed shouldn't bother you in here."

The three travellers let out a sigh of relief once they realised they weren't in danger, thanking Margaret and the other ghosts-turned-rescuers. Afterwards, she continued.

"Your other questions are harder to answer. People don't usually see us or even know about us. Even we barely know what and who we are. As to where exactly, well, I could not tell you exactly, we are on the roof of the Time Line, somewhere between Constantinople and—" At this point she stuck her head through the floor, peculiarly wiggled herself around and then popped back out again. "—Ooohh, a remote Chilean village of the Incas."

Pete's jaw almost dropped when she stuck her head cleanly through the floor as if the hard metal was the surface of a pond. He did not even ask how she had done that; surprises were coming at him so fast, and he had not fully recovered from the last one or the many before that. He looked at all the apparitions around him, and while most seemed to smile back, he noticed they were not smiles of joy, but rather politeness, hiding a forlorn acceptance of some grim fate. Pete started to feel sorry for these roof riders, something about them seemed like they had been through a lot.

"How did you get here?" Pete asked.

"Well, that's a bit of a long story, and each of us has our own to tell, all different and yet also the same." Margaret's mood changed, becoming suddenly distant and sighed, she continued in a defeated monotone, "We all tried to stop the demons, just like you, I suppose, coming out of that sky where Dezeptchen is causing his mischief. We all came from different places that we can't remember now. The demons came and caused their trouble and we tried to stop them. I don't even remember my family, only that I had one…"

A tear rolled slowly down her cheek, losing your memory couldn't be pleasant, Pete thought. She sniffled and resumed her tale.

"A few investigations later and we found out where they came from: The uncertain, unmapped lands, where the Time Line stretches out into everything and nothing. We went there and tried to stop them but then this strange curse befell us and now we have forgotten almost everything we used to know, including any information about our missions that might have helped. From then on everything is hazy, somehow each of us congregated up here. We can see others, but they don't see or hear us. So now we simply exist, half-alive, forgotten to both ourselves and the world, invisibly surviving on the top of the Time Line. Every once in a while, someone new tries to go beyond the Time Line's stations and they appear here. Now we sit and anxiously wait until someone can do what we could not – That is: to stop the demons."

Again, Pete had an unusual burst of confidence, and despite the miserable faces that stared at him from the ghostly crowd, he grinned.

"My two friends and I are going to do exactly that. We just need to get to Victorian London first in order to carry out our grand plan. Can you possibly help with this, Margaret?" asked Pete.

"I reckon you will be taken further than that before you are done, Pete, I really hope you succeed. But I will help you get to Victorian London first," said Margaret with a sad, knowing stare.

Soon enough, Margaret explained her plan to them. The only way to survive full Time Line warp speed was by being melded with the train in the way The Forgotten had been once their strange curse took hold. However, she explained there was a way around this using one of the strange tents that The Forgotten lived in, where they now sat after they had been carried in while unconscious, rescued just before disintegrating. Margaret told them that the tents were three-and-a-half dimensional, which had the advantage of tricking the way warp speed (and general spatial laws) worked. So, they simply had to stay inside the tent, while Margaret and her Forgotten squadron pushed them off the train, at the exact moment where they would be passing through Victorian London.

"OK, now we had better hurry... Victorian London will come in about two minutes," Margaret said. "Are you ready?"

Pete and Phil nodded while Reggie nervously scratched at his stomach, finally nodding along reluctantly. He was not so sure any more that he was enjoying all this adventure quite as much as he had thought he would. But... he had better go along in for a penny... in for a pound, he supposed. After all, he had committed himself to both helping Peter, and now also helping to get rid of the demons. Reggie was a lot more strong-willed than he knew, not the sort to break promises, especially to people in need. He realised that if he thought too much about all the things that could go wrong, he would not dare to go on, so he resolved to shake off his uncertainty for the sake of the greater good.

Margaret left the tent and Pete prepared for what he imagined would be a very hard collision with earth. As they all sat with gritted teeth and tensed muscles, Margaret poked her head back into the tent.

"Remember to keep this tent if you ever need it, it folds up quite nicely. Oh and—"

In a mix of excitement and anxiety, Pete interrupted, hurriedly thanking her for all the help. His nervous goodbye drowned out Margaret's last request, "Please remember us." Suddenly Margaret's head popped back out of the room and they could no longer see her.

"Oh, she was trying to say something; wait," Pete said. Pete rushed up to the entrance of the tent and pulled open the sheet to apologise and ask Margaret what she had said. Instead, he was welcomed by a wave of smog billowing into the room. There was no Margaret. It seemed they had landed in Victorian London just as she had promised they would, without feeling so much as a bump from the warp-speed crash landing. Once again, the strange tent had saved them. Pete reminded himself to thank… Oddly, it wasn't long before almost all memory of their saviours faded, all that was left was a niggling notion that they had forgotten something important. Although the sound of rapidly-approaching boots stomping on pavement meant that they didn't have time to feel guilty for being so selfish and absent-minded to not be able to recall those who had, just moments ago, saved them and helped them on their way.

Chapter 16
The London Kon-Troll

Following the smell of smog, eight baton-armed, blue-vested police officers jumped into the tent and seized Pete, Phil and Reggie, dragging them out into a city of brick, smoke and fire. As they stood, coughing and acclimatising to the polluted air, they saw huge factories surrounding them, their chimneys reaching off into the murky skies. They did not have much time to look around though, as they were immediately dragged in front of a laughably stocky man. He looked almost spherical but was broken up by ugly warts and lumps blistering out of his unhealthy skin. One of the policemen dragging Pete introduced himself as "The Controller."

"Well, well, well. What have we here, another bunch of freeloaders, eh? That won't do, no not at all." At this, he pulled out a huge roll of parchment that unfurled beneath them until their feet were all surrounded by mountains of old, yellowing paper with DA RULES!! written on the back. Reading the minuscule writing slowly and deliberately, the Controller continued: "Illegal use of train roof to ride without a ticket; dropping dangerously into streets by use of a three-and-a-half dimensional tent, extra penalty for disrespecting that I am in a bad mood on Tuesdays, unregistered presence of a clawed being without painting said claws purple..." He eyed Reggie suspiciously as he continued reading. The list went on and on as the rules they were breaking became more and more pedantic and outlandish. Finally, he ended with a harrumph and looked down his nose at the three so-called criminals before him. A spark of glee shot through his porcine eyes as he saw the helpless trio, surrounded by his baton-armed cronies, with nowhere to escape to.

"The minister himself will personally reward me for catching such dangerous villains as yourselves." Turning to his underlings, he said, "Two of you, resume carrying me, the rest of you, bring these scum to Minister Pauwer, would you?" The police squad saluted diligently. One of them had her back to the Controller while putting handcuffs on Phil, who was protesting loudly while thrashing about. Thinking she was out of sight; Pete saw her roll her eyes while saluting.

The Controller turned to the officer shouting, "Penalty for displaying exasperation on duty; you will be assigned punishment back at the station." A silent tear indicated the punishment would not be a light one. The police squadron shivered with terror and hurried to follow the Controller's orders to the letter.

They started getting dragged off, with police taking their arms and roughly shoving them forward. Meanwhile, two others strained to carry the Controller behind them, suppressing grunts that might offend their weighty taskmaster. He seemed to treat the arrest as if it were a gleeful procession at a carnival. Pete, remembering someone's advice, tugged on the tent with a flick of his wrist. It collapsed into a tiny napkin-sized square that was impossibly light. He quickly managed to whisk the shrunken tent neatly into his pocket, without being noticed, before he was unceremoniously dragged off.

After a little while of being dragged along like this, even Phil, after his initial struggles, was consigned to his fate. His initial kicks and protests were replaced by a sullen step with his head hung low. The Controller turned to them and said:

"Oh, don't look so miserable, you should at least be glad that I caught you and not... The Catcher. Let me tell you, they would not waste time bringing you to trial."

Even as he said those words, an ominous chill fell around the group.

"Who's the Catcher...?" Reggie whispered to the policeman holding him.

He answered with an even quieter whisper,

"No one really knows. All we know is that it is an evil creature who stalks the streets of London at night. Nobody is safe. It's why the people of London voted for Minister Pauwer and his promise to strengthen police authority. That thing, I hesitate to call it a person, could be hiding around every corner. No one has ever seen it and survived to tell the tale."

"Well, then how do you know that this Catcher really exists?" Reggie asked very sensibly. The policeman just looked confused and shot a brief, fearful glance up at the Controller, whose bulbous mass was still being carried along behind them. He was oblivious to the conversation, distracted by a greasy sandwich he had just guzzled down. Reggie never got an answer, upon seeing his boss finish his snack, the policeman was reluctant to participate in any further talk with the prisoners.

They all went back to staring at the cobbled roads beneath them, the smog filled up too much of the air, and they were not really in the mood to look anywhere but down. So, when the call from the Controller came, "STOP, STOP, HELP, HELP," it took them some time before coming to grips with their surroundings. It looked as if the Controller had just walked past an unlocked animal shelter. While he was being carried by the police officers, he continued snacking on an armful of herring. The smell of the fish had just been too much, and now there were cats all over him, clawing and scratching, purring and meowing. As the police around them realised the potentially devastating trouble they would be in if they did not immediately help their boss, they dropped their grips on the three adventurers and leapt back, trying in vain to remove the cats from the Controller. It was no use, for every cat that was pulled off, three more would jump down from the roof, or come tearing around the corner of an alleyway. Phil quickly took Pete's arm, distracting him from the comical and unlikely sight of a cat-attack.

"Come on, this is our chance, let's go."

They took their opportunity to sneak away into a dark alley, until finally the sound of raucous shouting and the innumerable screeching battle-meows faded into the distance. Although they were still perturbed by the arrest, they were very grateful to have escaped the Controller and his policemen for now. They definitely needed to be vigilant and keep their wits about them if they were to proceed on their adventure in Victorian England.

Somehow, they now needed to find directions to Muhammed Ibrahim Battuta's Victorian London contact. After the terribly tangled and strange streets of Impossibul, even the wiry winding alleys and cobbled streets of old London seemed to make perfect geographic sense. They were all grateful for a city that did not seem to move and shift after every corner.

After the previous odd experience, Pete started noticing a disproportionate number of cats roaming the streets. None of them seemed particularly vicious, however, and they did not bother the trio.

No hints of aggression indicated they could carry out an assault like the Controller and the police had just endured.

"Come on, we need to find someone who knows where this goggle-maker might be," said Phil.

"All right, Phil, but I think we need to be careful that we do not bump into this Catcher fellow that the police told us about. If they were telling the truth, it doesn't seem like the sort of thing you would like to meet in one of these narrow alleys," Reggie said, with Pete heartily nodding agreement at the suggestion of caution. With this in mind, they stuck to larger streets and away from all nooks and crannies, until eventually they got to a part of London where all the roads had evolved into wide avenues and the dark corners replaced by beautiful, well-kept gardens. The three cheered up at the sight of this less industrial part of town, as even the air felt cleaner and safer to breathe here. It was just what they needed after an awful lot of stress and trouble.

Confident that they were now far enough away from the Controller, Reggie spotted an old man close to where they walked and suggested they ask him if he might know any famous inventors, perhaps especially well renowned for their magical goggles. They approached the unassuming man, who was sitting on a bench just off the side of the road in a grassy field.

They stepped off the road and went towards him when suddenly they heard, "GETOFFFFF!"

The three stepped back in shock at the violent shout that the small, peaceful-looking man had mustered.

"I'm sorry, what?" Pete said as he approached the man once more, sure that he had misheard.

"GETOFFFF! GETOFF! GETOFF! GETOFF!"

Pete stumbled back as if he was physically pushed by the energy and volume of the shouts. Reggie tapped him on the shoulder and pointed to a tiny sign, far off in the distance, that only his raptorial predator-eyes had noticed:

Please: The Grass Here Has Been Tended by A Team of Highly Trained Professionals. Help Us Keep the Park Tidy by Never Using It.

Thank You.

Pete turned to the man and pointed at the sign.

"Is that why you are so angry?"

"The rules cannot be broken, it is how it goes," the man said, finally speaking at a normal decibel range.

"Is that your job then? You don't think you could get a bigger sign?"

The man began to cry, putting his head in his hands, sobbing apologetically:

"No... sniff, I'm stuck here. I, I, I didn't see the sign. I didn't see the signnn!" With this, he broke down into a tsunami of tears, crying so heavily that the salty droplets were falling from his face and staining his clothes.

"It's OK, just calm down and tell us what happened," Reggie interjected, feeling a pang of sympathy for the poor man.

"I, I, I was just walking, when the new minister was put in office. Then he made rules about stepping on the grass in all the parks, but it was already too late by then. I was in the middle of this field when the rule came into effect and the sign was erected. Now I'll be trapped on this bench forever." He stopped to wipe his tears and was just about to well up and go on another bout of hysterics when Phil ran onto the grass.

"GETOFF, GETOFF, GETOFFFFFFFF," the man said, a bit more weakly, but Phil did not budge, in fact he strolled closer to the bench the man was sitting on, all the while the man was whimpering his, "GETOFFS." Phil, who always liked a bit of troublemaking and rule-breaking, was enjoying his direct ignorance of being shouted at and stood right beside the man, wearing a massive grin on his face, while he extended his hand.

The man took it tentatively and was suddenly pulled up and onto the grass by Phil's disproportional strength. He looked at his feet in wild-eyed amazement, casting his gaze around 360 degrees. He could not believe it. He had not been struck down or arrested. He was breaking the rules and not in instant trouble. Then he and Phil walked back to the other two, slowly at first, with the man walking on tiptoes as if to touch as little grass as possible. But soon they could not contain themselves any longer, they started jumping around on the grass, running and enjoying the park's nature in this otherwise smoggy capital. By the time he was done exploring his newfound freedom and returned to Pete, it seemed the "old man" from the bench was twenty years younger. He thanked Phil repeatedly for showing him that not all rules were worth following. He now introduced himself to the trio. His name was Geoff, he said. Geoff Bell. The others introduced themselves. Once that was done, Pete remembered why they had wanted to talk to this man and now asked him if he knew of the inventor they were searching for. Geoff thought he did, having worked with an inventor on an eyewear-related project a few years ago. He kindly offered to lead them to the inventor's home as a way to show how grateful he was for their help.

"She is a bit funny and such. Difficult to find her, now she has gone in hiding, what with Minister Pauwer in charge and the Kon-Troll roaming the streets. Plus there is all that business with "the Catcher", so I can't blame her for hiding away," said Geoff Bell.

Meanwhile, behind them and unbeknown to them, a lamppost had been flickering on and off oddly, while slowly shifting closer to them, hopping along behind their backs as they walked. It followed them all the way from the park where they met their guide back into the bustling city centre, stopping to look like an ordinary non-animate lamp post whenever any of them glanced backwards.

Chapter 17
The Catcher

Their guide excitedly described the history of almost every building they passed, he was clearly very proud of his city, stopping only when the sombre effects of the recent events were made clear. There were signs everywhere, all with ridiculous rules scribbled on them; no walking on the right side of the pavement between 5:37 and 6:23, no picking up litter if it isn't violet or fuchsia, no helping people unless they didn't look like they needed any, and so on and so forth. Instead of protesting, the public response to these new laws seemed to be one of conquered acceptance. Most people had just given up and gone home, rather than risk imprisonment for some rule they did not know existed. As they walked past pubs, shops and theatres, Geoff would lament the lack of hustle and bustle. "Looks like it's mostly coppers and cats who are out and about since Pauwer's election. Not like in the good ol' days when people were outdoors, vibrant and happy." Sure enough, both were in abundance, just as Geoff had said. Police marched around the streets as if they were an army on manoeuvres. Meanwhile, a peculiarly large number of cats were prowling the rooftops, purring loudly and gathering in great congregations, looking down at the streets below them with conquering glares, as if plotting a grand coup.

After winding through alleys and avoiding police confrontation for some time, occasionally passing worried-looking people doing the same with their heads down, one crazed-looking young man shook Pete's shoulders saying, "The Catcher, he's here, he's close, ohh dear, why?" Then he skittered away before Pete could respond. Geoff assured them he knew where he was going, but they could see that he was beginning to get nervous, double-checking around every corner before they passed. They walked on in anxious silence, feeling their hearts racing as Geoff's visible fear was beginning to rub off on them. Finally, they got to an old building that Geoff said was the place. At least it was where he remembered the inventor lived before Geoff had gotten stuck in the park. As they stepped towards the house on the ominously quiet street, a screech came from the upstairs window and suddenly four more voices joined in, it was a cacophonous sound that grated the ears.

Geoff, at the back of the group, stopped suddenly in his tracks. He had heard the rumours circulating about the Catcher. The sound of screeching voices was supposedly the last thing the victims of the Catcher heard, before disappearing forever. Without thinking further in detail about how anyone would know that this was the truth, since the victims had supposedly disappeared forever, he panicked. He could not take it and ran as fast as he could away from the commotion, leaving his newfound friends alone to face the consequences. Pete had bravely stepped forwards, only glancing back to notice Geoff's hasty retreat as he was turning the doorknob to the house. He had a bad feeling about this. Geoff had seemed so nice and genuine. He wouldn't have tricked them and led them to a trap? Would he?

The door creaked open and Pete stepped inside gingerly, softly calling out, "Is anybody here?"

Silence.

"We're right behind you, Pete," Reggie confirmed. Gulping down their fears, they stepped into the house. Pete went in first and saw that the walls were covered in large multi-coloured eggs, all uniquely patterned and arrayed in neat rows on shelves that lined the entire room. Pipes and gears seemed to be sticking out of odd places, both in the floor and roof. Reggie was the last one in through the door. It shut behind him as a massive BANG came up from the floor below them and steam whistled out through the pipes on the floor. They all jumped in fright and then looked around in confusion as a massive horde of cats came running up from the basement stairs. There were so many that their movement blended with one another, looking like a single flowing wave of fur. Up and out of the house they ran, using every conceivable exit, flowing around the three investigators like a stream. This carried on for a long while, only when it seemed like more than a million cats had erupted out of the stairs, spilling like magma into the surrounding city, did the flow finally slow to a trickle before stopping.

The bewildered group was alone once more, staring with jaws agape at the stairway. Just when they thought nothing else was coming, a woman wearing a trench coat appeared, her long brown hair was covered at the top by a newsboy hat. She had a mad look in her eyes that was magnified by the huge, asymmetric goggles she wore, which made her eyes look mismatched, large and wild. She followed a straggling cat up the stairs with a smile on her face and a slight skip in her step. As she came to the last step, she turned towards the door and noticed Pete and the others for the first time, jumping back with a start.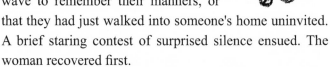

Equally, if not more shocked, Pete and Co were too dumbstruck by the cat wave to remember their manners, or that they had just walked into someone's home uninvited. A brief staring contest of surprised silence ensued. The woman recovered first.

"Well, you aren't the police, I can see that, so if you are not here to arrest me, why have you barged into my laboratory?" she said, holding her head up high, demanding an answer.

"Arrest you? Oh no, we aren't the police, no," Pete managed to stammer.

"Then what are you doing in my house? Strange to see

you walking around these parts, must be tourists then," she said. She gave them an analytical look up and down before continuing:

"Not afraid of The Catcher?" she emphasised, with an ironic grin. Pete was recovering his senses and managed to explain their quest and how Muhammed Ibrahim Battuta had told them to find the great goggle-maker of Victorian London.

"Goggle-maker, hah, Ibrahim is a lovely old crackpot, but he really does not pay much attention sometimes. I may have started my career as a simple magic goggle-maker many, many years ago but I have expanded my portfolio now. People call me many things; goggler, inventor, machinist, engineer, tinkerer, witch, chemist, magician. But most recently..." She dramatically paused for a long while, shooting them a very disconcerting lopsided smile, before finishing with a conspiratorial whisper, "The Catcher."

Reggie inadvertently stepped back at this revelation, while Pete and Phil took a step closer together in some sort of defensive formation. The Catcher laughed and spelt it out for them:

"C-A-T H-A-T-C-H-E-R, but you can call me Caitlyn. You see, it's my latest work of genius. People around here have let this awful new regime keep them scared for too long. Everyone is so afraid that they are unwilling to do anything about the situation. So, I'm organising a coup to get rid of Minister Pauwer and that wretched rat he sends to his bidding: The Kon-Troll." She looked at them as if everything she had said was obvious and clear. The puzzled looks she received told her otherwise.

"Let me explain it to you in more detail. I have a theory and a plan," said Caitlyn.

"I developed a cat egg laboratory, hence the name: Cat-Hatcher. But then Pauwer's propaganda made me out to be some sort of villain, as this suited his purpose in many more ways than one. On top of all the evil machinations and ridiculous rules they have been using to keep people submissive, they have also been spreading rumours that I'm The Catcher; an evil beast prowling the streets and something to fear. They used that fear to their own advantage, nothing makes the public willing to sacrifice their freedom as effectively as a good scapegoat. I suspect that "Minister" Pauwer and the Kon-Troll masquerading as the new police Controller are demons."

She continued, informing them, "I studied demons at a distance quite a while ago, with another of Ibrahim's friends at the Red Fort in Delhi, or Shahjahanabad, as it was called back then. This was before the Time Line was a one-way system when there were not so many demons, and they just used to cause mischief more than anything else. However, lately something very bad has been going on in all of Outermind, and I suspect it is because of the demons. The demons, who were previously little more than nuisances, have been getting more powerful and plentiful. While their little schemes of creating chaos and havoc have become grander and more evil."

"We're here to stop them too, that's why Ibrahim sent us to find you," said Pete.

"We need some goggles that can see through illusions,

that way we can rescue all the angles tricked by Dezeptchen and Kaoz in Constantinople. Then we can continue to help get all the demons under control," Phil finished, glad to finally meet someone knowledgeable on the topic of demons, who had the same mission as they did. Caitlyn did not necessarily understand the whole situation, but she trusted her uninvited guests. She fumbled about in an old drawer behind her and finally pulled out some goggles.

"Here, these should see through Dezeptchen's tricks. But I am afraid they won't be enough." She motioned to some chairs surrounding a small tea table in the corner. "Sit down, I need to tell you about my research, I think we might be able to help each other, if we pool our resources together and make a grander coordinated plan, we could take the fight to the demons and stop them for good, rather than temporarily patching up the problems they have created."

Meanwhile, unknown to Pete and his friends, outside the house they were being surrounded by an odd gathering of appliances including lampposts, fire hydrants and post boxes, they all clustered around looking no different than the others around the city, except they were marked with bright green paint that read:

"Do not tamper, property of Minister Pauwer. For the protection of the public."

They were tilting forward

slightly as if they were leaning in to listen to the goings-on within the building. One of the tall lampposts leaned down and tapped a small fire hydrant, seeming almost to whisper in its non-existent ear, whereupon it scurried off into the darkness.

Chapter 18
Pete's Quest and a Daring Escape

Caitlyn produced four cups of scalding hot tea, seemingly out of nowhere and they sat in a circle around the small table. Caitlyn asked Pete to explain in more detail how exactly he'd gotten here and his various run-ins with demons up till that point. It took some time to make heads and tails of this astonishing account, but she watched him passively and patiently while he explained, her eyes betraying none of the whirring theories that she was forming. When he was finished, she looked him dourly in the eye, saying, "So, you are not from Outermind but rather came through a mystery door? From another world, you say? Hmmm. You might actually…"

"What?" Pete asked impatiently, hoping someone would find an answer to his underlying fear that he may be stuck here forever, never finding a way back to his own reality. The answer he got was disappointing from that point of view, although it was good news considering his mission here in Outermind.

"You might actually be able to stop the demons, once and for all! You see, after much research, I have discovered where the demons originated."

She went on to explain: "They come from the uncertainty that lies at the end of the Time Line, a stop too far, a station too many. You will find the source of the demons there. You and only you will be able to get there. Everyone from Outermind who goes beyond the Time Line to stop them has never been seen again. I was beginning to lose hope until you told me how you saw through Feer and Diztruzt's curse when even the mighty Wikings could not, or about your mysterious saviours on the roofs of the Time Line carriages. That leads me to believe, in theory at least, that you have an ability to see things in a different way from most Outerminders. While it is limited by the trickery of the demons; I suspect Feer and Diztruzt got word to Dezeptchen and Kaoz of your arrival, allowing them to adjust their magic to your presence, though my truth-seeing goggles should counter that. Your otherworldly origin should allow you to bend the natural laws of Outermind, where the rest of us would break them. You have to get back to the station and go forward to save the future, past, and everything in between."

Pete couldn't believe, nor fully understand what he was hearing. He felt as if all the air in his body had been knocked out by a punch. All he wanted right now was to find a way home. He had enjoyed his adventure so far, there was no doubt about that, but now all these responsibilities were piling up on him. Every place he went here in Outermind, he seemed to stumble on new disasters and end up promising to help and sort things out. He worried that he was promising more than he could deliver... Did the people of Outermind know that back home he was just an ordinary boy, who had not even finished school yet? In fact, he felt so inadequate most of the time that he was often bored with who he was; spending his time imagining what his ideal self would be, or worrying about past moments where he could have done better, instead of actually accomplishing any acts of kindness. The adventurous spirit that had carried him this far had lost its whimsy and joy for discovery, replaced with a deep-seated fear of his newfound burden of responsibility. Worse was the fear of failure that came with it. His head started spinning when he thought of all the people he would let down and how it was surely better to just give up, instead of giving false hopes. Then he took a deep breath, determined to find new perspective before all the negativity took over: This time he had a chance to help, to finally be the hero he always wished he was.

Pete, you are so selfish. If you don't at least try, then you have failed before you've begun, he thought to himself.

Look at all the trouble people are in because of these demons. If there is any chance that I can stop them, then I need to help. I owe people here, like Reggie and Philosophocles. They have been nothing but kind to me. It's time to return the favour. He looked around at his companions, gaining strength and willpower from the kindness that they and so many others had shown him along his journey. Well, even if I am going to be stuck here, even if I might fail to stop the demons, I have an opportunity to help a lot of people, it's time I tried to do some good: For Elkie and her village, for Big Brigid, for Ibrahim, his princess and the people of Constantinople, for whoever saved us on the Time Line roof, for subjugated Londoners like Geoff and for all the creatures of Outermind being terrorised by those demons, thought Pete, feeling better with each hope. He wasn't going to stand by, paralysed by self-doubt, not this time.

The others were silent during this long pause, where Pete stared off into the air, looking lost and afraid. His breathing returned to normal, and he shook himself back into the present. Unaware how long they had been concerned about his moment of distant thought, patiently waiting for his answer, he simply said, "OK, I can do it."

Reggie patted him on the back, seeming to have some understanding of what qualms he had gone through.

"We'll be there with you all of the way, Pete. We are all in this together, the stakes have been raised, we won't turn back now you'll be needing help more than ever. After we stop the demons, we will get you home, Pete, don't you worry. We will find a way."

Just as Caitlyn seemed about to say something; perhaps a thank you or reassurance, the door to the room was kicked in. Splinters rained down everywhere amongst the delicate rows of cat eggs. (Pete was still getting to grips with the whole concept of cat eggs. Surely that was not a thing? Cats are mammals, they don't lay eggs, surely? Now was not the time to be asking biology questions though.)

"Owright, owright, nobody move." The heaving, pestilent bulk of the chief they had met earlier waddled aggressively through the door, flanked by two of his police officers, clapping their batons menacingly in their hands. Pete and his friends turned to the back door, looking for some kind of exit, but three more well-armed police, wearing bright blue uniforms pinned with badges advanced to block their escape.

"Just try and give me fifteen minutes or so, we need to talk to them and stall, I have a plan," Caitlyn whispered inconspicuously out of the corner of her mouth, just loud enough for Pete to hear.

The police slowly and menacingly formed a circle around them, inching closer until there was almost no distance between them and their captives.

"OK, lads, enough now. Come on, no need to make anyone uncomfortable," a decidedly cheery voice came from somewhere behind the police circle. The wall of blue uniforms stepped back to reveal a large, broad-shouldered man wearing an immaculate suit. He was grinning at the captives with a mix of cheerfulness and sympathy, something about his smile seemed very phoney.

"Hi there, I am Prime Minister Pauwer. Sorry about all this mess, but you are under arrest; general trouble-causing, rabble-rousing and the like. Oh, I do so hate to do this, but people like you force my hand. I do hope you won't take it personally and will still vote for me in the next election. I am granting suffrage to prisoners who agree with my policies." He grinned another winning smile, sparkly white teeth flashing, looking incredibly out of place next to the rest of the soot-stained Victorian Londoners.

"Troll, would you cuff them?" The Kon-Troll stepped towards them as Pauwer snapped his fingers.

"Wait," Pete said, stalling for time, remembering Caitlyn's whisper.

"Don't you have to go through a formal process to make an arrest? I thought you liked rules? And normal rules say you have to explain our rights to us, don't they?"

"Well, no, actually, I hate rules," Pauwer replied, winking conspiratorially and pulling a piece of paper from his pocket.

"That's why I am the only one who makes them," he cackled. He waved the paper in front of Pete's face that said: All police now answer directly to the Prime Minister. "And that's not all, I am sure you have seen my handiwork all over London. Hah! People are so confused they don't know what they can and can't do any more. They're all stuck trying not to tread on any cracks in the pavement or remembering what time they are permitted to do their shopping. In fact, they are so preoccupied worrying about breaking any rules, that they have no time or energy to challenge my power, just how I like it. If some upstarts like you think they can go around breaking all that and get away with it, then I always have the Kon-Troll and the police, right here in my pocket." He returned the paper to his pocket and gave it a pat. Some of the police around them grimaced a little, clearly annoyed by Pauwer's flagrant abuse of his position, but none moved a muscle to take counteraction.

"So, you realise, Pete," he said, emphasising the "P" just enough to lightly spatter Pete in frothy spittle. "There is nothing you can do, London is mine. Soon enough, I will take over the rest of Britain and then the world." He trailed off, cackling wildly, all traces of his initially amicable and calm presence gone, replaced with tyrannical madness that took over his false etiquette; his true ambitions revealed.

Meanwhile, all around London, the feline swarms the cat-hatcher had created were getting to work. They had commenced the first part of Caitlyn's plan: The cats had been going around systematically raking and clawing at all the signs, notices and warnings that Pauwer had put up. As they shredded into confetti, people's heads began poking out of windows. A few adventurous children took tentative steps out into the streets. Soon others began to follow; a trickle at first but it was not long before most of the previously homebound population was out on the streets, laughing and celebrating their newfound freedom. A march began; trumpets, tubas and all sorts of other instruments were played, for the first time since the new laws had banned them.

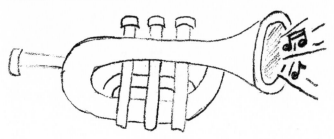

The rising swell of people began dancing and singing all around the swelling streets, while their subtle feline saviours slinked off back to the shadows and rooftops for the next stage of the plan. A revolution against Pauwer's abuses spread through all of London, secretly catalysed by a clowder of cats.

Back in Caitlyn's home, Pauwer and the Kon-Troll had no clue what was happening around the city. The police had handcuffed the four "criminals" and were bringing them to the Tower of London, where they were to be jailed. Little did they know that just down the street from Caitlyn's lab, waited a handpicked division of her canniest cats, equipped with custom-built commando gear. As soon as Caitlyn signalled them with two sharp whistles, they leapt at Pauwer, scratching and clawing at his fine clothing with trained precision. After a struggle and many shouts of "wretched blighters!" a cat wearing a beret pulled away from the melee, triumphantly clutching a little piece of paper between its teeth. A gasp went around the police officers, as all eyes turned to face it. It looked puzzled for a moment and then unceremoniously swallowed the little written rule that had been in Pauwer's pocket. Immediately, all the surrounding police breathed a sigh of relief, as if a massive weight had been lifted from their shoulders. Their lives were no longer in the evil minister's pocket and they quickly turned on Pauwer and the Kon-Troll, whose faces had now twisted into evil grimaces. The corrupt pair soon realised that their jig was up, and they were surrounded. Pauwer held up his hands in surrender but the Kon-Troll, who was looking more beastly than ever, bared his large meaty forearms, using his badger-like paws to dig: The thick claws that were not visible earlier made short work of the pavement and soon enough he was tunnelling at a rapid rate through the earth. Before anyone could grab him, he was gone, leaving a large, deep hole behind him. Pauwer capitalised on the confusion caused by this strange escape method and followed suit, jumping into the hole like a diver off a ship. A few cats attached ropes to their harnesses, rappelling down after them, meowing their fury at the close escape of their prey.

The police uncuffed Pete and the others, stuttering apologies and thanks. They left the alleyways behind, joining the growing parade. The police lifted the four above their heads, telling anyone who would listen that they were the ones responsible for their newfound freedom. Soon they were at the head of a procession that led them all the way to the Houses of Parliament, where a huge crowd had gathered. Caitlyn thanked the police and decisively strolled up, clambering on top of a pedestal displaying a bronze statue of an old king atop a horse.

"Oi! Everybody listen!" came a call from Geoff, who stood far taller and prouder than the jumpy and anxious person they had first met on the park bench.

"People of London!" Caitlyn cried out, and heads turned to face the pedestal.

"Prime Minister Pauwer and his Troll crony were demons, here to make all of our lives miserable. But now they have been stopped." A cry of cheer erupted from the crowd, but it was cut short as Caitlyn continued:

"Although they are no longer here in Victorian London,

we haven't gotten rid of them entirely. All over the rest of Outermind, these demons are terrorising innocents in the millions. We may have stopped these specific two for now, but they will always come back. Unless we do something to stop them permanently. To do that, I believe we will have to send someone to where the demons originated from. The lands of uncertainty, beyond the Time Line." A theatrical collective gasp rose from the crowd, a thousand mouths inhaling at once. Cries of despair rang out in the silence following the gasp:

"It's impossible."

"No one has ever come back from there."

"Who will do it?"

"It can't be done."

Caitlyn motioned for Pete to step up beside her. He looked around with uncertainty; secretly a part of him still hoped someone else would take over. Finally, he gulped and strode carefully up to the pedestal, until he rather clumsily failed to clamber up the tall, indented marble wall. Instead having to jump and take Caitlyn's hand, who helped pull him up. He felt very small standing next to the imposing bronze statue and Caitlyn, who seemed fine standing in front of the crowd. He was already imagining the crowd's disappointment when they were told that he was going to be the one to attempt this impossible task, he was the one who was supposed to save them.

"This boy is called Pete," Caitlyn introduced him with a flash of her hands.

"He is not from Outermind. He came here from another world. I think he is the key to stopping all of this, he might be able to go where no one has gone before. He has bravely accepted the challenge and kindly agreed to help us. For all our sakes we owe him our thanks."

At this a huge cheer, greater than any Pete had ever heard yet, assailed Pete's surprised ears. Chants of "Pete, Pete, Pete," and shouts of "Hero!" still felt as if they were due somebody else, almost making him look behind him for another person called Pete. Caitlyn smiled at him and mouthed a "well done," while the deafening crowd surrounded them.

"Well, nothing to it but to get back to the Time Line now then," Pete said to himself, in a voice that contained an odd mix of determination and befuddlement. Dazed by more fame than he could ever imagine, he clambered down to the floor, meeting an awaiting Reggie. Reggie wrapped his tail around Pete, preventing his stunned body from falling over. Meanwhile, Phil was playing security guard and very much enjoying this new role, excitedly telling people to back up and not crowd about.

They began to walk back to the Time Line station. By the time Pete had snapped out of his surprised haze and actually noticed some sensation of pride spurred by the cheers of the huge crowd, he was already boarding the train. He just managed to do a bit of waving back to the Londoners gathered outside the window before it sped off. Now he actually had to carry out the deeds that they all seemed to think he was the only one capable of; for which they were already cheering him as if they were certain he would succeed.

It was as if Caitlyn could read his mind because she

turned to him and said, "They aren't just cheering you because they think you will help them, you know. It's also because you have the courage to try, and they are grateful for that strength."

He was not so sure himself, but he thanked her anyway.

Looking up at the list of stops on the train, he saw only a few clear ones left, before a fuzzy line trailed off. In mismatched red letters that seemed to be moving and pulsing, he saw that the fuzzy line was labelled: Epochalypse.

Chapter 19
To the End and Its Beginning

Pete stared around him as they slowly ticked down the stops until the end. Had he just become used to it? Or was the once unfamiliar, weird and fascinating Time Line becoming more and more regular? Gone were the curious anthropomorphised creatures that clattered around during the jump from the Cretaceous to ancient times. Away was all the vibrant colour that sparkled brightly and danced along the walls. Now the only thing distinguishing this otherworldly transport from a regular train was the foreboding red letters "Epochalypse" inching ever closer to the little blip that marked their position. Everything outside looked dull as well, reminding Pete of his twice-daily school commute. He almost swore that he went past his hometown, in a flash that went by too fast to confirm the fact. Very quickly after that, things started to go wrong.

Pete, Phil, Caitlyn and Reggie were the only ones left on the train. Just when Pete had started missing the wackiness of the earlier Time Line trips, the increasing normality was shattered in a less wacky and more foreboding way. He quickly wished they were back to being in boring and normal surroundings. Within the space of a few minutes, Pete saw the world around the Time Line collapse into a giant sinkhole as the ground seemed to be pulled apart by invisible gargantuan paws.

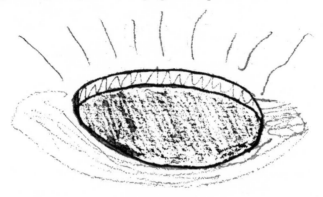

Then there was a colossal tornado, ripping the very earth up to the sky, flinging trees and buildings like grass and toy blocks. Then a flood; green, acidic water rising to towering levels, bubbling and bursting into toxic clouds. They passed empty towns, buzzing with pestilence. Volcanoes sped by; chaotically erupting with cataclysmic force.

All the while, Pete began to feel more and more wrong, like the sense of sniffing a glass of sour milk and knowing not to drink it. He saw the varied forms of devastation out of the window and knew he should not be here. But where could he go? This was it. He had made his choice and now he was trapped. No, it wasn't his choice, he started reasoning with himself, it was all these mad Outerminders, they had pushed him, they told him to do this, to be a hero. Well, he couldn't. He just couldn't. He looked around at Phil and Reggie suspiciously. Were they a part of this? Trying to get some poor lost boy from another world to do all their dirty work and clean up some mess they had made? Had that been their plan all along?

As if by some sixth sense, Reggie felt something was wrong with Pete and wrapped his tail around him, as he had so many times before during their time together. Pete shoved him away and balled his fists, glaring accusatively at him.

Just then, the group heard a loud DAKKA-DAKKA-DAKKA out the window and a familiar noise of helicopter blades slicing the air. A high-pitched squeal came from somewhere above the train carriage, they all looked in the direction of the noise, but the roof blocked their sight, obscuring the commotion. Right until a heavy thunk on the window and the sight of a sprawled creature in a suit, carrying an umbrella was clawing on the window. It was Diztruzt, from way back in their adventure, sailing with Brigid in the North Sea. He gave them all a vicious stare, mixed with pain, as he slid down the window and off into the turbulent landscape that surrounded them. Pete calmed down immediately, remembering all that his friends had done for him. The sight of Diztruzt tumbling into the distance put his thoughts back on track.

They all looked out the window to see if he would return. They saw the helicopter they had flown in earlier,

now with two large machine-guns attached to the sides. Muhammed Ibrahim Battuta was at the controls, saluting and giving them all an affirmative thumbs-up out of the window.

Suddenly a tidal wave rose up, large enough to easily engulf the helicopter and its pilot, faster than he could ever ascend to avoid it. Just as they all thought they were about to witness their friend being crushed and drowned in front of them, Ibrahim's eyes looked up at something on the roof of the train that they could not make out. Mere milliseconds before the tsunami ripped the battle-ready helicopter into pieces, Ibrahim jumped out of the helicopter, flailing in the air. In the nick of time, he was caught and enveloped in a hazily visible bag and yanked up to the roof. For a moment, all they saw outside was crashing water, one of the windows to the carriage started to crack. It was the first time Pete had seen any sort of blemish on the previously pristine Time Line. Just as they were starting to worry about the growing crack, the water disappeared. Now the window revealed nothing but a starkly dry and dead landscape before them. In spite of the colossal wave that hit the train mere seconds ago, the land looked as if it had not seen water in centuries. The ground was red and cracking apart, looking more like the surface of a distant planet than anywhere on Earth. There was not a living thing in sight, which added to the extraterrestrial quality of their surroundings. Finally, the train just stopped. No braking or slowing down, just a sudden stop that should have sent them hurtling out of their seats. It was almost as if they had never been moving in the first place.

Pete got up and moved towards the door, close behind him the others followed. He felt very apprehensive but knew that he had to go out there. Pete opened the door to the exterior of the Time Line, expecting a blast of heat, wind, or... something but none came. He hopped off the train and onto the dry, cracked ground. Little puffs of dust came from his shoes, as he trod on ground that looked untouched by living creatures. Looking around, all he saw was the train tracks stretching back the way they came and... nothing. That was all there was. He moved to the front of the train, seeing the tracks just end unceremoniously in the middle of this desert. He looked up at the roof and saw Ibrahim and someone stepping out of seemingly nothing and hopping down to join them. Seeing the hazy figure quickly jogged his memory; it was Margaret who had rescued Ibrahim with her tent, just like she had done before with Pete and his friends.

The group stood around in a confused and worried semicircle. The land was so flat, it seemed to swallow the horizon and the cracked, lifeless ground just stretched on for an eternity. A few of them opened their mouths to speak but the sheer dead landscape seemed to sap their thoughts and words. No sound came out until finally, a single confused sigh escaped from Philosophocles's parched lips:

"Huh..."

Chapter 20
Epochalypse

Lacking any better plan, the group set off back the way they came, hoping they could either find Diztruzt, or the remains of Muhammed Ibrahim Battuta's helicopter. As they walked, the ground started melting into darkness. All around them their shadows were cast in tendrilous winding patterns. The sun above started to shrivel and turn a sickly green colour. A soft cackling broke out, almost unnoticeable. The group started shooting each other uncomfortable looks, each of them starting to regret going through with this plan. Reggie thought back to his comfortable den, surrounded by green ferns and old friends. Philosophocles contemplated his great speeches back on the Acropolis, missing the adulation of the crowd and his scholarly peers' dedication to knowledge. Both hung their heads down, except for the occasional nervous look around. And Pete, regretfully he was missing being bored. Right now, the safety of his boring old classroom seemed blissfully comfortable. The surroundings were very frightening. For such a barren, lifeless wasteland the group still got the sense something was hiding, stalking them. Ibrahim and Caitlyn started uncharacteristically biting their nails, and Margaret seemed more transparent and otherworldly than usual.

Finally, they saw something during what seemed like an endless march into nothingness. It was the tidal wave that had crashed Ibrahim's helicopter earlier. It rose to disproportionate heights, growing quickly as they saw the huge distance between them start to shrink and the wave getting nearer to where they were.

"It's coming towards us," Caitlyn stammered. Her quick, confident voice replaced with a terrified whimper. Shouts of panic and terror arose, and the group froze in place. Pete pulled himself together, with a deep, calming breath and started to take a step. Or… he would have if he could move his feet. All around him, he noticed the others struggling to do the same to no avail, they seemed rooted to the ground.

"What's happening?" Margaret shook her stuck feet, having not been corporeal enough to freeze for as long as she could remember. None of them was able to move, they had been captured in yet another evil spell. A cackle arose in the air around them, and a sly, short creature in a doctor's coat approached them, just out of reach of their hands, giggling at their struggles to move. Taken aback by this insurmountable foe, the group looked at the demon doctor Feer, seeing various manifestations of truly frightening beasts with too many limbs, claws and teeth alongside him. Feer had brought a gang of his most hideous creatures with him in this final battle against Pete and his friends. All the while the tidal wave rising in the background was swelling and swelling. It was now only a few hundred metres away. Suddenly, the closest of the awful creatures that Feer had summoned was skewered on a massive, long harpoon. The creatures behind it followed suit, each punctured with slightly smaller (but still massive) projectiles. Neither Feer nor Pete and his friends knew what was happening. It was total mayhem. Nobody knew what to expect next. A whoop suddenly arose from atop the tidal wave. The group, now absolutely cowering, putty in the hands of Feer's evil machinations, looked up at a Viking Longship, majestically cresting the wave, hundreds of metres above their heads. Feer saw the vicious harpoon attacks on his creatures, finally getting a taste of his own medicine, he quaked with fright. Seeing his plans unravelling, he squealed a pathetic shout of cowardice. The tables quickly turned. Feer disappeared, sinking into the sand. Suddenly they were released from their frozen positions and Feer's evil spell. Once again able to think as the haze of panic lifted, Margaret shouted at Pete:

"The tent!" Pete reacted quickly and understood what Margaret intended, pulling the little square of fabric out of his pocket, he held it by a corner and shook it vigorously. It immediately formed into a full-sized tent.

"Everybody inside!" Margaret and Caitlyn shouted simultaneously. Just in the nick of time, they all managed to enter the tent. Phil was the last one through, and just as he was zipping shut the opening behind him, the tidal wave hit, spurting litres of water into the tent. Pete jumped up to help Phil close the tent, pushing through pressurised water that sprayed forcefully into their faces, they managed to close the tent before it filled up. Immediately after fully closing the tent, everything went quiet and peaceful as the outside world seemed to phase away. The only thing reminding them of the terrible danger outside was the layer of water that sloshed up to their waists.

A massive beaming smile greeted them as they cautiously reopened the tent.

"Brigid," Phil shouted exuberantly, running to hug the oversized woman. She embraced them all in one massive reach of her arms. They stepped out of the tent onto the deck of The Whooping Wanderer once more. They saw all of Brigid's Wikings holding the same nets they had used to ensnare Elkie and her brothers, now used to hoist the tent to safety. They whooped and cheered and greeted with their signature exuberant bear hugs. The group couldn't quite believe what had just happened. They had been saved just in the nick of time by Brigid and her Wikings.

They tentatively stepped onboard the longship and continued sailing the mysterious wave across a lifeless desert, the Wikings expert sailing skills somehow kept the ship steady with precise manoeuvring. They could find no sign of Feer and the other demons. Pete looked off the side of the boat and could have sworn that he saw strange faces in the purplish ooze that formed the wave. They were wearing every possible emotion from misery to joy, but just as their features became clear, they were engulfed by the wave and replaced with new faces. The still wind and the dead landscape stretched eternally beyond both the longship's bow and stern. The sheer force of this massive wave seemed starkly out of place, especially when the group remembered their energy-sapping walk across the cracked ground. While the wave seemed to be moving quickly, it was hard to tell how far they had actually come when everything looked the same. Brigid called for one of her crew to take the rudder and strode over to Pete.

"What is your plan, Pete?" She asked a bit brusquely; used to giving commands, not asking questions.

Pete looked back at her, slightly shocked and also worried at being thrust into the role of decision-maker. He did not really have a plan to speak of. He had hoped what they must do would be made clear once they found where the demons came from. Instead, everything had only gotten more confusing and disorienting than even the rest of Outermind.

"I suppose we keep going?" Pete answered very quietly, not providing much reassurance.

And then the ship did something very odd; it started to fly! Pete looked around and noticed that the massive wave, which had been constantly threatening to engulf them, was no longer heavily rocking the longship. All that was ahead of them was the stark blue-grey sky as the ship tilted up into the air. The Wikings collapsed to the deck, sailing the treacherous tsunami had tested even their mighty nautical prowess. This illusion of flight soon ended, however, as they were hit by a sudden sinking feeling. The boat was not flying at all, instead it was plummeting downwards.

Pete ran to the side of the boat to get a look and saw that the "wave" beneath them had all but receded, replaced by a massive pancake-shaped blob that seemed to be gurgling at them. There were faces forming in the blob matching the ones Pete had seen in the sludgy foam earlier. They were starting to coalesce; creating one large, looming grimace that seemed set to swallow them all as they fell towards it.

"Boinggg." Just as they were all braced for impact, the ship once again launched up into the air, bouncing off the ooze below. Reggie was immediately sick with the upheaval and ran to the side of the ship. Below them they heard a bellowing gurgle, shifting constantly in pitch and tone, making it very hard to understand.

"Remember me?" Out came a low moan that echoed unpredictably. The voice then fired off in a set of explosive blasts: "Kaoz, Kaoz, Kaoz," then it shifted to a mock apology:

"Oh gosh, I am so sorry, I ought to set you down now."

"Or maybe I won't!" Kaoz said triumphantly.

Now speaking in the voice of a cruel tyrant, it bellowed, "It's time to stop playing."

Kaoz changed course once more, finishing in an unnerving, high-pitched tone, "Noooo, we like to play, time for them to flyyy. Fly up and away and meet our friend." Then he engulfed their ship in one oozing grasp and flung them high, high up in the air, leaving the formless blob of purple alternating between delirious laughter and crying sobs of simultaneous joy and sadness.

While the others panicked and cowered, Phil looked off the side of the temporarily airborne ship, almost feeling bad for the mad anomaly that had launched them. Then he saw a truly magnificent sight: their saviours. A large flock of gold-feathered gulls flew to their rescue. The flock of gulls all worked in unison, taking hold of the ship and its crew, suspending them in mid-air; temporary relief from Kaoz toying with them, or so it seemed. Phil was not sure where this was all leading, or for how long the gulls would be able to suspend the ship. Off in the distance, he also saw a figure coming towards them. His doubts were confirmed; it was only temporary relief.

"Uh oh. No one look!" he managed to shout, before falling to his knees and averting his eyes.

Chapter 21
Deceived, Defeated and All Alone
at the End of the World

Dezeptchen's beautiful metallic figure floated towards the ship on angelic wings, when it saw Brigid and some of the Wikings ready their weapons, it shot them one long disapproving look, and they immediately dropped them passively. The group of meddling adventurers before him fell to their knees in praise. Once again, the demon's evil spells were working, and once again Dezeptchen had them in its bewitching charm. All it had taken was one look at the "angelic" creature and they were enthralled. Not quite all of them though: Pete was faking it! He had put Caitlyn's goggles on just in time. Through their truth-seeing lenses, he saw Dezeptchen differently from the others. Floating ahead of the ship was no golden reflection of goodness, but in reality, a dark, impish creature, cackling and rubbing its slimy hands together. Looking down, he saw the formerly extravagant birds beneath them revealed to be an ugly mess of decomposing bones holding them aloft. Unlike the others, Pete was able to see things as they truly were, instead of what this apparition intended to appear before them.

Margaret was enthralled by the same trance as the rest but had a distinct sense of deja vu. She had been in this exact situation before. Although it was a distant, forgotten memory, just like everything else that had happened before she found herself on the Time Line's roof. Then Dezeptchen started to speak, and she stopped trying to recall the past in order to listen to the great words of this supposed angelic figure. Dezeptchen began to point at one of the Wikings.

"You, my sweet children." It singled them out one by one.

"Away you go, you will be forgotten forevermore." As it spoke, each person it pointed to disappeared with a "poof", gone in the blink of an eye. The last Pete saw of his allies were lopsided smiles of worship gawking at Dezeptchen, until their final flash out of existence. Dezeptchen continued in this fashion while Pete watched helplessly as his friends all scrambled to be the next one to receive this "blessing". Like stars in the night sky approaching morning, he saw everyone he had met along his journey vanish. Reggie was the last to go, and finally it was just Pete left, sitting on an empty ship, all alone. Dezeptchen completely ignored him, as if he too had disappeared with the others. Pete did not quite understand. He watched as the impish figure slowly floated away, complaining how much of a hassle it was to banish pesky

Outerminders playing at heroics.

"Why do they continue to try and stop me? They must know it is all in vain," it cackled.

The ship slowly sank through the air, as if it were barely suspended by spiderwebs. Pete hopped out once it finally reached the ground, hoping against hope that he would find his friends waiting for him. No such luck... He was now all alone in this hostile wasteland where demons played cruel games, using unfortunate visitors as their toys. Finally, where all the other obstacles had deterred him, this last crushing loss of hope did something unexpected. Instead of giving up, Pete got angry, invigorating him into taking action. These demons had taken his friends and almost his sanity, they had caused trouble one time too many, and he was getting just about sick of it. He shouted as loud as he absolutely could, the sound echoing across the abyssal plains that stretched out all around him:

"Come and get me then! Here, you missed someone, you stinking, filthy demons!"

His shout rolled around him, another grim reminder of just how isolated and alone he was. There was no response. Pete took one last glance back at The Whooping Wanderer, it looked incomplete and defeated without its crew. It's tattered sails and patchy hull was more reminiscent of a long-lost wreck, rather than the majestic longship that had deftly surfed a hundred-metre demon-wave mere moments ago. He stepped off the ship, aimlessly wandering once more; this time alone with nothing but his thoughts. He kept shouting around him into the surrounding wasteland, mostly for his own sake rather than intimidation. He had no expectation that any demons were bothered to listen.

Chapter 22
Hope and Restoration

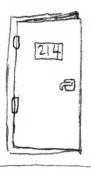

Pete forced himself to stay determined; imagining himself single-handedly defeating all the demons and saving Outermind, then being cheered through the streets again and maybe another helicopter ride in celebration. He thought back on his journey and all the odd shenanigans that had transpired. He thought back to meeting Muhammed Ibrahim Battuta and the confusion of Impossibul, his mad idea to draw an L-shape that had actually worked. This brought a sneaky smile to his face. Thoughts began to rush through his head, and he focused his imagination: If demons could change a whole village to seal-creatures, convince all the angles in a city to take to the skies and enslave Londoners by inventing ridiculous rules, then maybe, just maybe, Pete could do some invention of his own. He closed his eyes and considered the future, previously its uncertainty had always scared him, with all the ways things could go wrong, the setbacks that could make life miserable. He took those fears and turned them on their head; uncertainty turned to excitement, negativity to positivity, he stopped dwelling on all the ways the future could change for the worse and imagined all the new possibilities it could bring: Music to hear, books to read, sights to see, new friends to meet, the adventures he could have, inventions that seemed like magic, the knowledge to learn, and all the joyful moments in between that make life worthwhile. The demons that stood in the way suddenly seemed much smaller and insignificant in comparison

When Pete opened his eyes, he saw the desolate landscape around him start to shrink. A distant hill quickly diminished to become a small bump beneath his feet. Pete started wondering whether he was growing massive, or if everything else was shrinking around him. With his newfound determination, he now strode along with a purposeful gait, each step covering what would previously have taken hours of travel. A whizzing noise whistled in his ear, and he got the sense that something very hard and very fast was approaching the back of his head. Just managing to duck, a familiar chalky "L" hit the ground in front of him. For an animated letter embedded into the ground, the "L" seemed to give off a lot more energy than its simplicity let on. Pete yanked the "L" out of the ground and remembered his satisfaction when creating it. He began to swing it about like a samurai. It whooshed satisfyingly as it cut through the air. Pete felt a little better with every swing, soon he was almost skipping along, humming a tune. Something seemed to be going right for the first time since arriving in this twisted place at the end of the world. With each step, with each hum and each dance-like swing of his "L", he became more and more certain that his hunt for the demons would be a success. Earlier he feared his friends would be lost forever, defeating the demons was a matter of revenge, now he had a far better motivation; he was coming to their rescue. The blistering march through the cracked desert turned to more of a summer's day stroll as the nuclear green sun went back to its usual bright yellow, warming him instead of burning.

Finally, way off in the distance, Pete saw Pauwer once more. After his escape from Victorian London, Pauwer had found his way back to his fellow demons. Another few steps and Pete could see that Pauwer was standing on a makeshift stage, leading a meeting with his kindred demons. Well, he was trying to. These evil spirits seemed much harder to organise than the people of London, it seemed their powers were useless without a hint of morality among them; there were no hopes to corrupt, no fears to prey upon and no order to manipulate. Feer was trying to trick the rest into listening to him by inventing threats that only he could save them from. Pauwer was trying to enforce a voting system where his voice counted for ten. Meanwhile, Kaoz was loudly shouting from four different mouths, saying four different things, disrupting the whole process. The Kon-Troll was busy trying in vain to capture Kaoz's amorphous body, and Diztruzt was in the corner, changing his mind every minute, never staying on the same side for long. Dezeptchen stood apart from the rest, focused on his recent conquest over another band of do-gooders, more interested in gloating than agreeing on anything. The others were trying to figure out their next plans of action to cause more misery and how to avoid the mysterious boy called Pete, who had foiled their last attempts. Feer, always on the lookout for danger, real and imaginary, was the only one who noticed Pete approaching.

The boy who they had thought was little more than a nuisance now towered above them, dwarfing even Dezeptchen's grandiose form by an order of magnitude. Feer screeched and pointed, biting his nails in a panic. The rest ignored him, thinking it was yet another attempt at diversion. From their position high on a craggy rock cliff, the demonic council had a full view of everything that was happening in the Epochalypse. Still, they were far too busy arguing to notice Pete striding towards them, until his massive shadow cast them into darkness. After some curmudgeoning, Pauwer managed to yell the diverse demons into a concentrated group, slithering, crawling, buzzing and sneaking towards this interloper. What on earth was he doing in their lands, trying to stop all their ruinous fun? This would simply not do. No way. This was not part of Pauwer's grand plan, nor that of any of the other demons.

Pete looked towards the varied ghastly beings that were advancing towards him. He remembered all the things he had gone through to get here. With each memory, good and bad, he lost a little of his fear facing the demons. Seeing his reaction, they all gave him a slightly confused look, quickly covered up as they returned to their cruel glares. Pete was momentarily lost in a glimpse of happier times, stifling a little giggle as he thought back to Reggie's snoring which shocked a roomful of scholars engrossed by Philosophocles' mad ranting lecture. His mind wandered back to the desert again, he saw the demons had stopped mid-charge, looking around confused. Their momentum was lost until Pauwer managed to yell another order:

"CHAARRGGEEE!!!"

He was followed by supporting chants, "YEAH, GET 'IM!"

But despite the volume of the demonic shouts, they seemed a little bit... unsure, and not able to take action. Feer and Diztruzt stopped moving towards Pete. In fact, it was as if they were slowly retreating or standing still, while pretending to be running full speed towards him, hoping the others would take the risk. Even Kaoz and Dezeptchen, who had no reason to fear Pete, were moving very uncertainly, even though they were closer than ever and Kaoz had shifted to a tendrilous form with sharp hooks. Soon they too had stopped, and neither of them really seemed to know why. Pauwer and the Kon-Troll broke out into visible terror. Moments ago, they were the ones giving orders here, convinced Pete would baulk from their assault. So, what was going on? For the first time, Pete saw the worry behind their sneering masks of superiority. Were they really just as scared of him as he was of them? No, it couldn't be, they are dastardly demons, it must be some sort of ruse. Finally, he readied his "L" like it was a golf club, now easily large enough to send all the demons flying in one great swing. Just as he was about to smack them senseless, he reconsidered, violence would only feed evil creatures like them, making them stronger. So, he did something unexpected. He gave them a wide, dismissive grin, reaching from one cheek, stretching all the way across to the other. Somehow, he knew they couldn't hurt him if he ignored them and prioritised more meaningful goals than fighting. It was far more important that he save his friends and undo the damage the demons had done to Outermind, rather than vainly trying to destroy them. He remembered Caitlyn explaining how they had always existed in the dark corners of the world but only recently gained enough power to cause devastation. It dawned on him that stopping the demons was not possible through traditional means, instead it was a matter of weakening their influence and making them as insignificant as possible. He suddenly knew what he had to do, rubbing his hands together he got to work. He saw the Epochalypse for what it was!

The empty, lifeless surroundings were simply a product of the demons' desire to create a miserable wasteland for themselves, where they could thrive and stew in their own negativity. But Pete knew now that no part of Outermind belonged solely to the residents of these little slices of time and space. Outermind was a place that all formed together into one whole where everyone gives a little bit of themselves to shape one continuous through-line; nowhere existed without the input of those who came before and those who would come after. It was a place that could and should thrive on its residents working together and for the most part, they had done this. He refused to allow the demons to ruin that wholeness with their cruel intentions. He looked at the wasteland that lay at the end of it all and no longer saw a hopeless husk but a blank canvas.

Pete opened the floodgates of ideas in his mind to this cracked landscape, feeding it with positivity; exactly what the demons had denied the lands for so long. Tropical colours began to blossom, starting with small flowers of every hue bursting up through the bitter, dry crags that divided the earth. Soon whole rainforests were springing up with the renewed hope emanating from Pete's thoughts. This place was going to be a lot nicer from now on Pete determined, knowing that doing so would "complete" Outermind and have a knock-on effect to improve the rest, all the way from here to the Cretaceous. He looked back at the demons, who now seemed almost comically small. Dezeptchen's gleaming gold body did not carry the same sway when it could be fit into a matchbox. Even to the last, the demons could not simply let this happen. Gathering the tiny demons together, Pauwer quickly attempted to make one last desperate plan with his fellow demons. The plan was hard to hear, given how small the conspirators had become to Pete. It seemed quite obvious that they once again disagreed though, as the demons started pushing each other out of the way to be the fastest to escape. Only Kaoz remained, although something had changed about the odd mad blob; it seemed cheerful, excited about the changes around him, as if it had been released from some pressured captivity the other demons had trapped him in. Maybe even demons had good sides to them; Pete wondered about that for a long time afterwards. The rest were running away, trying to escape from their very large enemy; however, they had no need to worry. Pete was now more preoccupied with finding his friends. Now that the demons had lost their power and were revealed to be as insignificant as they were. He was not at all bothered with catching them. He started walking back to the Time Line, happy to realise his sense of direction had returned. When he got to the tracks, he noticed they no longer stopped dead in the Epochalypse, it seemed the whole transport system had not just been fixed but significantly upgraded. There were multiple tracks and platforms, now going every which way imaginable; new visitors were flowing into the landscape that was no longer terrifying. Kaoz had returned to normal size and was greeting them like a tour guide:

"Welcome to The Future, where anything is possible, follow me, everyone! These lands are more unstable than the rest of Outermind, I will make sure you do not get lost on your visit."

Pete explored the platforms, considering where he should look for his friends, feeling a slight pang of regret seeing all the interesting places he missed along the way. Although he was also glad to know that there were still endless possibilities for new adventures. He did not have to look for very long. He came to a platform that was decorated with all sorts of festive regalia; there were balloons of every colour, laurel wreaths and beautiful bouquets of flowers that originated from all over Outermind. The next train arrived at the platform and Pete saw it only had one stop… and his name was even on it!

Fast train to Pete's festival.

He approached the opening doors, the mysterious conductor welcomed him personally:

"Come on, Pete, get aboard. I've made this ride especially for you. Wouldn't want to keep everyone waiting, would you?"

Pete looked around in vain for the source of the conductor's voice, it seemed to come from invisible speakers that ran the length of the platform, as well as the train itself. He gave up and stepped on board. He barely sat down before falling into a deep, well-deserved sleep.

He woke up to a chorus of cheers, the train had stopped somewhere familiar judging by the ancient ferns that grew right up to the window. He stepped off the train onto a hastily constructed wooden platform and was hit by a wall of humid, rainforest air. He yelled a thank you to the train as he left, hoping the conductor could hear him, wherever they sat.

"My pleasure, Pete, I should thank you for fixing the Time Lines! Now enjoy your party!" the disembodied voice called back as the train zoomed off this new platform into the thick jungle of the Cretaceous. He turned around in the direction of the cheering and saw Reggie's house, built between two massive ferns. Close by was a simple, classroom door, matching the one to his maths room. It stood in the open, conspicuously not attached to anything. He was back where it all began.

Standing behind the door was a whole host of joyful, celebratory denizens of this strange place that Pete had so quickly become quite attached to. They were all whooping, yelping and celebrating in the ways they knew best. A primeval thrum of growls, roars and snarls thundered from the creatures of the Cretaceous, singing together they created quite a chorus. The sounds of lyres and pan-pipes drifted down from a ramshackle amphitheatre that the Ancient Greeks had hastily built. Here Pete recognised many of the faces (and strange inventions) of the crowd at Phil's lecture at the Acropolis. There was now a lake behind Reggie's home that Pete could have sworn was not there when he first arrived, from it came bellowed chants from a familiar-looking ship, loudest voice of all coming from Brigid, clutching proudly to the figurehead of The Whooping Wanderer. Muhammed Ibrahim Battuta led a chorus of Constantinople/Istanbul's citizens in a rhythmic chant that made the air itself vibrate with the volume with the sound of hundreds of voices, they were obviously glad to have the angles return to their city, some even waved giant chalk-coloured L-shaped signs reading:

"Thank you

P

E

T

E

!"

Pete couldn't find Margaret and The Forgotten, until he saw a crowd near the lake wearing slightly soggy clothing, there stood Elkie and her younger brothers, now returned to human form, next to them was an older girl who shared the same distinguishable fire-red hair and freckles. The girl waved and smiled at Pete in a way that reminded him of

Margaret, she must have been their lost sister. The sight of their reunion and the whole Viking village free from their curse gave him a rush of pride. He had fulfilled the promise he had made to Elkie, back when he first saved them from Feer and Diztruzt! Caitlyn the cat-hatcher played a grand organ with meticulous, practised perfection, a well-trained team of felines assisting her to strike chords no one could play alone. Looking amongst the various crowds from the cities of Victorian London, Constantinople and Athens and many other places he had not visited, he saw unfamiliar faces, who he still recognised somehow. The Forgotten were forgotten no more and had returned to their families, bringing them along to celebrate their saviour. The sight of their grateful smiles took away any lingering doubts he had, confirming the Time Lines had been fixed. All the brave adventurers stuck going "beyond forever" to stop the demons, had found their way to their respective homes in all manner of places. He had done it, he really had! He'd stopped the demons and mended Outermind! All it had taken was some self-confidence, a bit of hope and help from a lot of very good people along the way, to conquer the corrupting pessimism the demons had spread. Their influence had shrivelled by refusing to believe the hateful powers they emanated could shape the world. Could it really all have been that simple?

Overjoyed that, despite all the doubts along the way, he had kept the promises he'd made to help this mysterious world. It was difficult to imagine that he had once seen Outermind as an uncertain and alien place, with all the fondness he now had for its marvellous weirdness and colourful inhabitants. A part of him still knew his own world was waiting. He too needed to find his way home… Pete looked about at all the cheers and merrymaking that surrounded Reggie's humble house, once again noticing that oddly conspicuous classroom door, which jutted out of the ground right in the middle of it all. He took a few slow, deliberate steps towards it and turned around. He had a feeling that he should say goodbye before fulfilling his last wish, he didn't know when or if he could come back once he stepped back through the door to his world.

"Thank you all for teaching me so much." The crowd settled down, listening intently to Pete's nervous speech.

"It's been a really marvellous adventure, it really has. The kind of adventure I never could have dreamed of. I can't quite put my finger how, but I feel different somehow… It's a good sort of different, I don't think I'll see anything the same again. The future feels full of hope and exciting new experiences. I can't imagine I was ever bored when I still have so much to do, and I have you to thank for showing me that! Especially you, Reggie, and you, Phil. If you hadn't stuck by me all this way, I don't know what would have…"

He was not used to showing his emotions or talking in front of crowds, so Pete looked down at his shoes while he spoke, trailing off before his nerves paralysed him. Then he looked up hesitantly, although once he saw there was no judgement, but rather sympathy and understanding on the crowd of smiling faces (and cheery eyes from those without faces to smile with), his tension melted away. Reggie and Philosophocles stood right at the front of the crowd. Pete looked them in the eyes, and they began to step closer, knowing the time for goodbyes had come. Phil began bawling shamelessly, while Reggie allowed a few dignified tears to drop down his goofy lizard face. Pete embraced them both, and the strange trio, who had been through so much together, made their way right to the handle of the door, where the fantastically weird adventure had begun.

"Will I see you again? What will happen to this door when I go through it? It wasn't always there, right? What will you do while I'm gone?" Pete asked quickly, making the most of these last few moments together with two of the kindest, wisest beings he had ever known.

"So many questions, my boy." Reggie let out a bittersweet chuckle. "That's good, you stay curious now, Peter, it will help more than you know. And don't you worry about us, we will be fine, especially now that you put the demons back in their place. I suspect that door will disappear, just as it appeared when you first arrived, but I wouldn't worry if I were you, I'm sure you'll find a way to see us again." With that, he winked and turned the door handle; opening up a passageway that led into Pete's classroom. Pete took one last look round, making sure to memorise all the creatures of Outermind.

Phil wailed hysterically, "We'll miss you, Pete. Good luck with everything."

"I'll miss you too… thanks again for all you've done," Pete replied.

Then he made up his mind. No more time to hesitate. He stepped through the classroom door and slowly closed it behind him. The sounds from the farewell party shut off immediately. Not much happened once he walked back into the classroom. Time was still oddly frozen. The teacher was in the same position mid-sentence, everyone sat just where they were before Pete's whole adventure started. He wandered over to his chair, as strange as all the time-stopping and otherworldly adventures had been, Pete looked at the stopped clock and was no longer worried that he had gone mad. He looked at the books on the desk in front of him in a whole new way. They were so much more than just "boring" books, suddenly they had all become portals to understanding. He was intrigued by the teacher's markings on the board. Even maths (which used to seem a bit pointless) was a treasure trove of possibility now. His adventures had made him realise how important knowledge could be. With his newfound sense of excitement, he considered how he might use this moment where time froze to read all the books, learn all there was to know, and then he would be ready for anything. Just as he wondered how he might do that and considering whether being ready for anything would be boring, without any exciting surprises, the clock started ticking:

Tick Tock

Tick Tock

Movement erupted around him, pens started clicking, a paper aeroplane soared across the room, the teacher stopped to yell at the thrower, and as soon as that interruption happened, a dozen whispered conversations started up. The chaos that used to be so bothersome now comforted Pete. He started to grin, not even realising he

was doing so. Life was never going to be boring again, that
was one thing he knew for sure.

The End

Made in the USA
Middletown, DE
22 June 2022

67131365R00097